# Big Doc's Girl

# Big Doc's Girl

The Classic American Novel By

# Mary Medearis

*August House / Little Rock*

PUBLISHERS

**Library of Congress Cataloging in Publication Data**

Medearis, Mary.
  Big Doc's girl.

  Summary: When misfortune comes, Mary, daughter of a doctor in rural
Arkansas, becomes head of the household and sets aside her romantic
dreams.
  [1. Arkansas—Fiction] I. Title.
PS3563.E2385B5  1985     813'.54  [Fic]  84-45641
ISBN 0-935304-87-8 (pbk.)

Previously published in hardcover by J. B. Lippincott Company. The hardcover edition is now out of print.

Second August House Printing, 1989

ISBN 0-935304-87-8

  This book is printed on archival-quality paper which meets the guidelines
for performance and durability of the Committee on Production Guidelines
        for Book Longevity of the Council on Library Resources.

  AUGUST HOUSE, INC.     PUBLISHERS     LITTLE ROCK

Cover design by Byron Taylor
Design direction by Ted Parkhurst
Typography by Al's Typesetting, Livermore, CA

# Big Doc's Girl

# I

THE BACK COUNTRY of Arkansas is always the same, no matter which fork of the road you follow. Always the narrow, rutted wagon road winds through thick woods of pine and scrub oak and sumac bushes; always past green and white cotton fields, tall waves of whispering corn—down the same valley, up the same hill, in at the gate and along the path to the weary, rain-grayed farmhouse.

And it is always the same woman waiting on the porch. Always the same man who brings you a drink from the well. His shoulders are the width between the furrows in his field, his skin is sun-drenched as the earth, his eyes as naked as the rain, his words as simple as his being. The plow in the soil, the lash of the storm, the coming of spring—that is the man and the back country. They were sired in one, dust of dust, flesh of flesh. . . .

Our house was built at the edge of the town when I was six and Little Doc was four. Big Doc, our father, stood under the big oak tree in the corner of the yard and said, "We'll build here, Myrtle. You can have the front door for your piano pupils from town, and I'll take the side door for my patients back country." Mother nodded, and the house was built.

It was a big square house, set back on a wooded slope from the dirt road. Mother had always wanted a yellow house, Father had always wanted a green one—so the top story was painted yellow, the bottom story, green. There was no fence, no gate. Not a tree was cut that didn't need to be cleared for the foundation. That left a giant sweet-gum tree towering directly in front of the three porch steps—but who cared what the amused neighbors thought? One of the two bedrooms over the porch was my room, and there were leaf patterns to dance on my wall during the nights of the moon, and ice-laden branches to scratch music on the front porch roof in winter.

Father's sign was at the side door: "DR. R. S. CLAYBORNE, M.D." Mother's sign was at the front: "MRS. R. S. CLAYBORNE, PIANO TEACHER."

The years wore on and the signs grew chipped and scarred. Our house had become the dividing line between the town and the country: there was always the piano pupil at the front door, always the man from back country knocking at the side. I watched them all from the screen of branches outside my bedroom window.

Two little sisters were growing up in the house during those years—Melie Kate and Ruth. They grew into pigtails, new front teeth, school-books. . . .

Then one spring they were eight and six, I was sixteen, and Little Doc only lacked a month of being fifteen.

The March wind came in that year, blustering and blowing up to the living-room windows as it had done so many years before. It found me where it had no doubt always found me—sitting on the fourth step behind the banisters, listening to Mother give a piano lesson at the big black piano at the other end of the long room.

It was late afternoon: Billy's lesson was the last one before supper. I had heard three lessons since school was out, and now I turned to look out the window on the naked black trees bending in the wind, the glow of the sun as it disappeared beyond the distant line of hills.

March had chosen a glorious day to arrive. The sun had been warm, the air sharply cold and good to feel. Now the sun stood poised on the brink of the horizon, looking back on the trees and fields, and the wind that swooped with a shout around the house.

Suddenly the wind and the space enfolded me, holding me close to its bosom, lifting me high in the vast arc of time and space. I was essence of clouds, color of the sunset. The wind roared and laughed around me. Somewhere I touched a feeling. "Something has begun to happen!" I whispered—but the wind swept the words into thunder that echoed and re-echoed in the empty dome of sky. "Something has begun to happen! Something, somewhere has begun to happen!" Swiftly I clapped my hands over my ears. "It's imagination!" I tried to shout against the towering wind. "It's all imagination. . . ."

I merely sat on a stairway, a piano lesson going on behind me, a cold March sunset before me. The wind was gone—the horizon was a dull golden glow.

Mother's footsteps sounded behind me as she walked across the floor and said goodbye to Billy at the front door.

"Did you say something to me, Mary?" she asked, as she closed the door behind him.

"No."

It was getting cold at the staircase, now that the sun was gone. The living-room would be deep in shadow at my back.

Mother switched the light on. "You may have a lesson now while I get supper, if you like," she said.

It was a moment before I answered. "I haven't practiced very much."

"You'd better let me hear it anyway. I won't have time tomorrow evening."

Her footsteps tapped briskly on her way to the kitchen, and the stove door squeaked open as she lit the oven. I stood up with an effort: sitting on the step for so long had made my legs stiff and cramped.

"Do you want to hear the Chopin first?" I called out to her.

Her voice came muffled from inside the pantry. "Either that or the new Beethoven. Whichever you feel like."

I went to the piano and took my music from the bench. Imagination or no, there was a strange cold feeling around me tonight. Something had happened out there in the sunset and the wind. I needed something to grasp hold of again. Perhaps the Beethoven Sonata.

But there was not even security in Beethoven tonight.

"Oh, Mother, I can't!" I cried out to her. "I can't play anything right now. Let me go to the corner and meet Father. I'll help you dish up when I get back!"

The oven door squeaked open again and the heavy iron skillet of corn-bread was slid in. "Go ahead. You can play tonight when you've done with your schoolwork."

I ran out the front door, through the darkening woods, on up the road to the corner of Maple Street. Father's car was due to turn down from Main Street, a block beyond, right on the stroke of six. He would see me—Little Doc and I used to wait for him every evening when we were small.

Now I stood, breathless and shivering without my coat. Of a sudden I could hardly wait for the car to come. I wanted to see Father—his twinkling gray eyes, his bony awkward hands, his long swinging stride as he walked before me into the house.

When the car finally squealed to a stop beside me, I opened the door of the front seat and climbed in quickly.

Father chuckled. "Are there a couple of ghosts behind you, Sissie?"

"No. I was afraid I would miss you."

"Don't go out this way without a coat again," he said. "This is flu weather."

"Yes, sir."

We rode the short block home in silence. Grayness was settling down:

the north star gleamed faintly over the chimney. Now that it was evening, and Father had come, everything was right again. The sunset had happened a long time ago.

The car stopped under the extension porch and Melie Kate and Ruth came tumbling out of the house and onto Father.

"Papa—look what Ruthie did! She fell in Pat's fishpond and she's got a bump on her head!"

Ruth was indignant. "It doesn't hurt! I told you it doesn't hurt, Melie Kate!"

"We'll take her in and put her in a sling anyway," Father said, picking the two of them up under his arms.

He strode up the terrace, around the sweet-gum tree and set Melie Kate and Ruth down on the front porch. "Something smells good," he said, opening the screen door. "Is it the lye hominy that I've been making?"

"It is not," Mother answered from the dining-room door. "This is Friday night. Treacle and brimstone."

Father rubbed his hands together. "In that case I'll wash up and be right down. All the little boys in Dickens had to wash their hands and slick their hair before they got their spoonful of treacle and brimstone."

He set the medicine case on top of the bookcase, then took the stairs two at a time. I went to the kitchen to help Mother dish up supper.

The table was ready by the time Father came back downstairs again, his footsteps clumping in the old rubbers that were his houseshoes. He had on the baggy, motheaten suit that he always wore when he hoped to spend an evening at home.

"Three evenings at home in one week, Robert?" Mother said when she saw him. "Have all your patients left?"

"Nope. I'm spoiling my wife."

Mother snorted, and I laughed. He would be asleep in his chair by the fire, long before Melie and Ruth were finished with their schoolwork.

We bowed our heads for grace. The back door slammed, footsteps ran across the kitchen and Little Doc slid into his chair just as Father began the first words of the blessing. "Our Father—" The rest was a jumble. We had never been able to piece out the words from there to the "Amen."

Heads were up, and Father reached for his napkin. "You nearly skinned your nose on the deadline this time, Son," he said dryly.

"Yes, but Dad, you ought to see my rabbits!" Little Doc's face was flushed from cold, and his voice was eager. "Nine new ones born last night. Sired them by the big buck we caught in the woods during the snow."

"He didn't wash his hands," Ruth said righteously.

Little Doc held them out. "I did, too. There's a faucet at the side of the house, Missy."

"Sister." Mother's voice came quietly from under the other ones. "Sister, you forgot to put the salt on the table. Get the new cellars in the pantry."

At I left the room, I heard Melie Kate say, "Little Doc's got a girl."

"So has Freddie Harris," Little Doc answered coldly.

I was back in the dining-room as Melie Kate blushed to the roots of her hair. "He lives down this way, Mother, that's why he walks home with me. He lives right down Maple Street."

"In a green house," Ruth supplied.

"That's fine," Mother answered. She handed Melie Kate the bowl of grease beans. "Pass these on up to your father."

"What's the matter with Sister?" Little Doc asked. "She hasn't said a word since we sat down."

"Nobody's given me any room," I said.

"She'll say something when I tell her who's going to be here Easter," Father said.

"Who's going to be here Easter?"

"Dr. William Barrett Sheehan."

"Bill!" We all shrieked it at once. Bill hadn't been back since he had taken his year as resident surgeon in St. Louis City Hospital, the September before. When he finished there, he was going to return to go into practice with Father.

"Mother, you'll have to get Jenny in," I said, excitedly. "We'll have apple strudel and ham for dinner."

"We'll have ham only if Jess Johnson remembered to bring it in," she said. She looked at Father. "Did he?"

Father nodded. "Half a hog." His eyes were on his plate as he added, "and a bushel basket."

"Robert!" Mother's mouth was a straight line and she laid her fork on her plate. "Robert, if you let that man bring another bushel of turnips— I swear that if he brought so much as one turnip, I'll stand right there by that door and belt him with it the next time he comes for you. I've eaten the last turnip I ever intend to."

Father roared. "It's peanuts!" he said.

Ruth was so tickled that her elbow hit the spoon-holder, and the holder, spoons and all went crashing to the floor.

In the laughter that followed, none of us were sure that we had heard a knock on the door. It came the second time before we were certain of it. Then our laughter was stilled and we all looked at Father. The knock on the side door only meant one thing—the man from back country stood there.

Father laid his napkin on the table, pushed his chair back and strode over to the door. "Yes?" he said, as he unbolted it.

The man stood in the square of light at the foot of the steps. His face was sweaty and dust-grimed from a long journey. He motioned behind him with his hat. "I got the woman in the wagin . . ."

Father stepped outside and closed the door behind him. His rubbers clumped down the stone path to the wagon.

"Pick up the spoon-holder, Ruth," Mother said. "The rest of you go ahead and finish your supper. He might be quite a while."

But Father was back before Ruth had finished gathering up the spoons. He stood by the side door and spoke to Melie Kate and Ruth. "Take your plates upstairs to finish eating."

Ruth set the holder back on the table, and the two were gone without a word. They had done this before. When their footsteps were on the stairs, Father spoke to Mother. "It's a maternity case. No chance of getting to the office or the hospital."

"Sister's room is ready," Mother said.

Father's voice was terse. "Better fix the table in the living-room."

He went out the door again and Mother turned to me. "All right, Sister. Little Doc can help me."

I ran quickly to the closet under the stairs, for the rubber mat and sheeting. They had served to make our long oak table into an operating table many a time before. This was the first time for a delivery table, however.

I had to work fast. My fingers were thumbs, but the last of the strings were tied around the legs of the table when footsteps came around the corner of the house. I grabbed the medicine case from the top of the bookcase and closed the dining-room door behind me.

The kettle was almost ready to boil in the kitchen. Mother brought two white-enamel pans from the pantry, and laid them on top of the oven to put the instruments in to be sterilized. Little Doc took the case from me and opened it.

The steps were on the front porch now—two pairs of men's footsteps, slowly bearing a heavy burden between them. The front door opened. Then, later, released from the burden, one pair of footsteps went back across the porch and in another moment a whip cracked and the wagon rumbled around the front and up to stop by the trough in the corner of the yard by the oak tree.

"They'd water their mules if it was the crack of doom," Mother said impatiently. She thrust a package in my hands. "Take this in, Sister."

I went back to the door into the living-room and knocked. "Father!"

"Yes?"

His voice was hard and abrupt—an eternity away from the one at the supper table.

"Here's your apron."

The door opened, Father took the package from me, and the door was closed again, but in that brief instant I had seen beyond to the woman on the table. Her body quivered with child, her work-reddened hands gripped the sides of the table until the knuckles were white. There was agony in every curve, every line.

I stood there a long moment by the crack of light at the door. Father's rubbers made a squishing clump as he walked across the floor. There was no other sound. When Mother came from the kitchen with the steaming pans of instruments, I opened the door for her, then went back to the kitchen. "He forgot to take his rubbers off," I said to Little Doc.

The minutes dragged by. There was nothing for us to say or do. We could only wait to be there if we were needed. Little Doc spread a newspaper on the floor and started whittling on a stick of wood.

"A boat?" I asked him, finally.

He held it up. "No. A totem pole."

Upstairs there was a padding of bare feet across the hall. "Maybe I'd better go up and see that Melie Kate and Ruth get to bed all right," I said.

When I came back downstairs again, Little Doc wasn't in the kitchen. His knife and totem pole lay among the wood shavings on the newspaper. Standing still to listen, I heard his voice in the living-room, over by the stairway. "Which chair, Mother?"

"The cane-bottomed one," she answered.

The heavy silence of the house was oppressive. I took Little Doc's leather jacket from the peg by the stove and went outdoors to sit on the back stoop.

The air was clean and cold. The northern cross glittered brilliantly in the sky by the edge of the woods. I breathed deeply, but the heavy empty feeling was still around me.

Restlessly I got up from the stoop and went around the side of the house to see if Jess Johnson's bushel of peanuts could be in the back of the car. The two windows on that side of the living-room were blank rectangles of light. Not even shadows beyond.

The basket was in the car and the lid wasn't nailed down, so I filled my apron with peanuts and started back around the house again.

A match flared at the side and a cigarette was lit. Someone sat on the garden fence rail. It was the face from the side door—but this was no man! He was only a boy.

I walked over to him. "It's chilly out here. Won't you come in?"

A cloud of smoke went up against the night. "No, thank'ee, Ma'am."

I stood there, hesitantly. What must he be thinking, with those two long rectangles of light before his face and no sound anywhere but the raucous shrill of the cicadas and the creak of the tree frogs?

I swung myself up on the railing beside him. "You're Haskel Wilkins," I said. "You were here last spring with a bullet in your shoulder."

He blew another cloud of smoke. "Went skunk shooting."

I laughed. "I know. Father said that the skunk came in with a bullet in his leg that same evening."

The man chuckled. Then all was still again. The north star gleamed silver over the chimney.

He motioned with his cigarette toward the two rectangles of light. "How's she doin'? Heerd anything?"

"Not a thing, but don't you worry. She'll be all right."

"I hain't worryin'," he said. "Big Doc'll take keer of 'er."

My heart filled in my throat. What ease there was in his voice when he said, "Big Doc'll take keer of 'er."

He said, "Tom Glazer back country said yore Pa went acrost the ocean to git his paper to frame."

"He studied until he got four papers to frame. Paris, London, Vienna, Rome—"

He drew in on his cigarette speculatively. "Four, eh? She'll be all right, I reckon. This is her first 'un." He leaned his elbows on his knees and said, "I heerd, too, that Big Doc's years older'n Miz Doc."

"He's twenty years older," I answered. "He was forty-five when he found her."

"I warn't but seventeen when I stood up."

Seventeen! And this their first child!

"How old is your wife?"

He crushed his cigarette on the fence rail. "Sixteen, now."

Something quivered in me. No older than I. Of a sudden the back country was here, hard and solid in the grip of my hands. This was what my mother and father walked in. This was what supper was left waiting on the table for. The suffering on the table, the words on the fence. My mother's quick footstep in the kitchen—those great awkward hands of my father that held the suffering and faith of the whole of the back country in them—his stark gray eyes with the laughter behind them, that wept the only tears I ever saw there when he had to amputate the leg of a boy whose legs were only meant to walk a furrow from sunrise to sunset. You, man on the fence beside me, you don't know how great the hands are that are delivering a son to sweat and push a plow for you!

The rectangles of light were suddenly blackened. It was finished, and I would be needed. I left without a word. The peanuts spilled from my apron.

In the kitchen, Mother was stripping the rubber gloves from her hands. "You can help Little Doc in the living-room," she said.

The light was on again, and I went in. Little Doc stood by the table, bare now of the rubber mat and sheeting. He spoke to me. "Do you know why he brought her in in the wagon, Sister? He didn't have but eight dollars. He wouldn't ask Father to come twenty miles out for that."

But my eyes were on the table, at great long scratches in the varnish. Deep scratches, made by fingernails.

I looked up at Little Doc. His eyes were as naked gray as Father's had ever been. "She didn't make a cry," he almost whispered to me. "Not a single cry. She said, 'Don't worry, Miz Doc. We won't wake your little ones.'"

# II

SATURDAY MORNING AFTER Good Friday, I sat on the front-porch swing, watching the rain thrumming down in a silver sheet. It was only after breakfast, but the sky was as dark as dusk. In a moment Father would be leaving for his rounds back country. Little Doc wasn't going: he was in bed with flu.

The screen door was flung open, and Father strode out. His hat was jammed low on his head, his overcoat collar turned up high about his ears. That was Mother's work—left to himself his head was always bare, his coat unbuttoned and flying out like bats' wings.

"Father, could I go with you?"

He was brusque. "No, no. Not this time."

"Please. It's been years since I've been."

"You stick to your piano."

He always said it, so there was no need asking more. He started the car and backed it from the extension porch. The rain made it look gray and distant: it was difficult to distinguish the sound of the motor from the wind.

At the edge of the yard the car stopped, and Father leaned out the window to shout through the rain. "Hurry up! Get a coat!"

"Yes, Father!" I shouted back.

The swing bounded wildly behind me as I jumped to the porch floor, and ran in the house for galoshes and raincoat from the closet under the stairs.

"I'm going with Father!" I called to no one in particular.

Out the door again and across the yard to the car door that was open, waiting for me. "Look at that!" I laughed, breathlessly. "I'm as bad as Ruthie, with my galoshes on the wrong feet."

Rain drummed on the roof of the car as we headed for the pike, and out the two miles to the turnoff where the dirt road began. There the car jolted and slid in the slick ruts deep in rain. The road wound and curved through woods and fields and lowlands. Occasionally a weatherbeaten house showed grayly through the wind-curved rain. Once, when it slacked, I wiped a place on the window and looked out.

"Father, look!"

"Can't take my eyes off the road."

"It's beautiful. There's bare hill, with a naked tree against the gray sky."

"That's a dead landscape. Why don't you pick one that breathes?"

"It's not time for those yet."

Father gave a short laugh. "An oracle from Ecclesiastes sits beside me. 'For everything there is a season, and a time for every purpose under heaven.' "

I said, "I'll tell you something that Mother thinks is beautiful."

"What's that?"

"Coffee in a cream cup on a yellow saucer."

"I like to smell the National Geographic Magazine."

"I like your old Shakespeare better. And the inside of old houses. I love to smell Aunt Melie's house."

"It always smelled like mice to me."

"Little Doc likes the smell of cotton when it's being ginned below Clendenin School."

"How about the smoke and dust after a train passes?"

"I can't think of anything but the bell when I see a train pass. Every time it whistles past our crossing, I want to drop everything and run after it as hard as I can go."

"Well, sir—" Father's voice stopped in mid-air, and I knew a story was coming. "I ran after a train whistle once. I was grubbing mesquite in Texas. Next thing I knew I sat in a dormitory room in the Arkansas University, studying Greek and Calculus. Couple years later I heard a steamboat whistle down the Mississippi—I walked out without my hat, and there I was in Paris, in the Latin Quarter, cutting up a frog for a dissection class."

"So, ad infinitum, sic temper fugit, and I became a doctor's daughter."

"Well—your Mother was in on it."

"I don't know. She says I sprang from your brow like Jupiter's daughter."

Father's roar matched the wind. Then suddenly he stepped on the brakes and the car stopped with a jerk.

"Scott! Look at that!"

I wiped the moisture from the windshield to look out. In front of us was the narrow bridge over Cooper Creek. The tiny little stream had become a torrent of swirling yellow water. The backwash was far up on the road, the waves washed over the planks of the bridge.

"We can't cross that," Father said.

"Do we have to?"

He hesitated. "I ought to get over and see about Cull Brant. Jess Johnson says he's down with malaria again—he won't call when he's got no money to pay."

I waited for him to decide.

He turned to me. "Want to wait here or come with me?"

"I'll come. How far is it?"

"About a mile as the crow flies. We can get across the footbridge a piece down."

He backed the car off the road and up on a mound in case the water should rise higher. We rolled the windows tight shut, then Father took his medicine case from the back seat and opened the door on his side of the car.

"Ready?"

"I'm ready."

The rain beat on us with a windy roar. I kept my head down and my eyes on Father's feet. He headed for the river bank, then down toward the footbridge. Water rushed by in a torrent beside us. The trees beat their stiff black arms together: another week and their winter torpor would be gone, and spring sap would race through their veins. Grass would be green after this rain.

We reached the old stone bridge. Father turned and shouted above the wind. "Ever cross a flooded creek by a floodgate?"

"I've never even seen a floodgate."

"Here we go, then."

He turned and strode through the wind again. I wanted to shout with the exultation of the noise and motion around me, but the wind was pushing hard against me and it took all my strength to push back again.

A quarter mile down and we reached the floodgate. Below a ramp of stone hung a wooden-slatted gate, swinging back hard against the heavy onslaught of water. The water burst with a roar beyond, foaming over the stones and on down the swollen creek. There must have been a great storm farther back in the hills—the water was full of yellow mud and driftwood.

Father stepped up on the ramp and reached up for the thick cable that anchored the gate to trees on either side of the bank.

"Careful," he called back to me.

I was too breathless to answer.

Father's steps were slow and surefooted. I followed slowly, my hand sliding carefully along the cable. I daren't look down; the roar and spray of the water was dizzying enough.

Father stopped and turned. "I nearly drowned once doing this," he yelled. "Had on brand new brogans, too. Pa shook the water out of me until I couldn't stand up, then he whipped me till I couldn't sit down." I didn't dare laugh. I was afraid of losing my balance.

Father reached the end of the ramp while I was still several yards behind. He let go of the cable and started to jump to the bank below.

Then suddenly I saw his foot slip on the wet stone. His hand clutched frantically for the cable and it lurched in my hand as he caught it. Slowly he pulled himself up. In a moment he stood on the ramp again, and my breath came free.

But something was missing! The medicine case! It bobbed like a big black cork in the swirling water below. The current had already washed it far from Father's grasp. It was whirling toward the middle of the stream. Another moment and it would reach the heaviest rush of water, past the big stones and debris that were trying to hold it back.

I watched, petrified, as the case swept around the rocks and broken limbs. A sapling brushed over it and pulled it along toward the floodgate.

Then I let go of the cable and lay flat on the ramp. If the sapling turned over in the water there was still a chance. It was heading straight under me. I reached my hand down as far as it would go. It wouldn't quite touch the limbs of the sapling. I edged over a little further.

There it went! The water gave a mighty lurch, the sapling rolled and turned as it pushed against the floodgate, and the medicine case was thrown high in the waves. I couldn't reach over far enough—only my third finger curved around the handle! A longer arm than mine reached down and lifted the case from the water, just as the tree rocked and pushed and was gone through the floodgate.

Father stood up and helped me up beside him. The case dripped in his hand.

I laughed shakily. "I hope it's waterproof."

He started to answer, then changed his mind. He turned abruptly and went down the ramp again. I followed more quickly this time. The water seemed to have lost much of its fury.

Father stepped carefully from the ramp to the muddy bank, then reached back to help me down.

"Won't Little Doc really look sick when I tell him that for once in my life I crossed a high creek and didn't fall in?" I said.

"Hey!" Father shouted, reaching for me, but it was too late. My foot had slipped and I had gone backwards into the slimy, yellow backwash. I sat in water up to my waist.

The half-mile on to Cull Brant's house seemed two miles. My shoes squished dismally: my feet and legs were icy. There was no excitement in the wind and rain, now. It was only cold and monotonous.

The house finally appeared around a bend in the road, and Father led the way through the gate and up the path. The front door opened when we reached the top of the steps. Cull Brant's wife stood there—big and warm and brown in the chill grayness.

"Come on in, Big Doc. Some rain, hain't it?"

Her tone was as matter-of-fact as if we had just come from across the road.

"Some rain," Father agreed, in the same tone of voice. "How've you been, Lizzie?"

"I'm doin' just fine."

Father stomped his feet on the gunnysacking on the porch. "Thought I'd come by and show you my girl."

The woman glanced quickly at me, then away again. "Pleased to know ye." Then, to Father, "No one said ye was a comin'. We'd've cleaned up a bit."

"We can't stay but a minute. I've got to get on down and swab out Tom Glazer's tonsils again." He took off my galoshes and set them by his rubbers. "Some day when he's not looking I'm going to cut those tonsils out of him. Every rainy day I have to come running out."

The woman laughed.

Father reached for my coat but I shook my head. He hung his on the peg by the door and we went in.

Not a trace of the gloomy day was in here. The room had a glow that smelled of soap and sunshine. The floor boards were slick from countless scrubbings. The black iron stove, the table by the wall, the ancient hall rack, the two straight chairs and the rocker—all were as polished and dustless as a new shoeshine. The woman, Lizzie, seemed as little a part of the room as the day outside. Her shapeless dress was soiled and faded, her shoes rundown and flyspecked. She was far away from the cleanliness of the room, and yet so heartily and earthily a part of it. These people had always given me that odd feeling.

Father walked over to the big black stove and rubbed his hands together over the heat.

"Where're the boys?" he asked Lizzie. "Setting out rainbarrels?"

"They're out to the barn. Bessie's bringin' in this mornin'."

"Cull there, too?"

All at once the woman busied herself with the two straight chairs to face the stove. "Cull's sick," she said.

"Malaria?"

She nodded. "He ain't bad off enough to call you yit, though," she said, her eyes still on the chairs. "We aimed to call ye if he got yaller black agin."

Father said, "Think I'll go in and talk to him."

"He's in the bedroom thar. I put him to bed with a poultice." She raised the lid of the stove and peered inside. The fire was gold on her face. "Ye kin walk on in, I reckon. He ain't asleep." The lid closed and her face was brown again.

Father strode over to the door and into the bedroom. He left his medicine case behind. I felt, more than saw, the woman look at it.

She motioned to the chairs by the stove. "Ye kin sit down thar if ye want to."

"Thank you."

The wetness of my clothes was like layers of ice on my skin. The fire was beginning to crackle; the sound made me shiver.

A door opened in the room in back. The wind blew it shut in a sound of rain, and there were footsteps in the kitchen.

Lizzie raised her voice. "Birdie?"

"Yes'm."

"Come in h'year a minute."

More footsteps and a girl about my age stood in the doorway. Her face glistened wetly from the rain, her clothes were as soiled and shapeless as Lizzie's.

"Birdie, this h'year's Big Doc's gal."

"My name is Mary," I said.

The girl half smiled. Then she flushed. "I ain't clean."

"Look at me," I said. "I fell in Cooper Creek. Father says I get goose-grease on the soles of my shoes every time I come to a footbridge." I tried to laugh, but my voice ended on a shaky shiver.

For the first time, the woman, Lizzie, turned and looked squarely at me. "My goodness!" Her voice was sharp with surprise. "Yore plumb soaked! Pull thet cheer up clost to the stove."

She came over to me and pushed the chair almost onto the stove before I had a chance to rise. She sat on the other chair and reached for one of my feet. "Let me look at them feet. And don't you worry about this old dress none, young'un. Hit's dirty already."

My shoe was off and her big warm hand closed around my foot. "My goo-ooodness! Wet plumb to the marrow! You must've fell clean in!"

"I did." Suddenly I was shaking from head to foot.

Lizzie pulled the muddy stocking off and reached for my other foot.

"Birdie, see if they's any hot water left in the cookstove. Git some towels and a blanket, too."

All shyness had disappeared from the room. Lizzie was bustling efficiency. Birdie smiled fully at me and turned back to the kitchen. I heard the heavy iron stove lid set aside, the rattle of a dishpan.

"Put it in the stewpail," Lizzie called.

"Hit's full of perserves."

"Well, git the biler then. Git it in h'year quick!"

Birdie was back with the pail of water, and floursacking towels around her shoulder. When Father came from the bedroom a few minutes later, I sat swathed in blankets, my feet red as lobsters in water so hot that it steamed up to my face.

Father looked at me and chuckled. Lizzie's voice was cutting. "I cain't think of no better way to git pneumonia, Big Doc. Let me look at yore feet."

"Send me a bill, Lizzie, send me a bill."

"Let me see them feet!" Her mouth was firm.

"I had on overshoes."

"Thet don't mean nothin'."

He walked over to her and held one foot up. "Dry as a bone."

She nodded, satisfied.

Then Father picked up his medicine case and set it on the table. His face was serious again. "Now I'll preach you a lesson, Lizzie. Your man's full of malaria again. Why didn't you call me?"

Defensiveness was in every line of her body. "He ain't yaller sick yit."

"He tells me he's had three chills."

Her mouth didn't change, but I could see her eyes and they said something else. Father held up a bottle of brown liquid and a box of pills.

"I'll swap you these for half a cord of wood," he said, looking hard at her.

She only looked back at him.

Finally she said, "What kind of wood?"

Father set the bottle on the table and closed the medicine case with a snap. "Well, now, that depends. If that much medicine and one hypodermic don't get him up by cotton planting time, then he can bring wormy pine. If he feels like entering the county tree-chopping contest, he can make it hard oak."

Lizzie grinned. "Hit'll be oak."

Father turned to the girl. "Get me a pan of boiling water, Birdie."

He took the hypodermic case and went into the bedroom again. In a moment Birdie followed with the pan of water. Lizzie pulled up the rocker and rocked wordlessly until Birdie returned. Then she said, "Reckon ye better git some clothes fer Miss Mary to put on. They'll be fixin' to leave in a little bit."

Birdie went to the kitchen and opened a door into another room. When she came back, her arms held a roll of clothes that she put shyly in my lap. She stood behind the stove, and I looked down at the garments. They were new. They smelled of sachet and a cedar chest. The underwear was of soft white lawn, with hand-done stitches as infinitely wrought as for a wedding garment or a baby's dress.

"Oh, Birdie, I can't take these—" I said, holding them out to her.

She backed farther away behind the stove pipe. "Them're the ones I went fer," she said.

Lizzie's chair creaked across the floor boards, and I put the clothes back on my lap. I tried to say "Thank you," but the words were too inadequate. "Guess maybe I'd better get ready, then," I said, instead.

It was late dusk when we reached home. The rain had almost stopped. There was a light mist and will o' the wisps in the fields. The day had been a long, busy one, and both of us were tired.

Mother met us at the front door.

"I'll have two in bed with flu after this," she said crossly. "You knew better, Sister."

Her face looked more tired than usual tonight. Her forehead had a frown, and there was no amused quirk to her mouth.

"I'm sorry, Mother. I thought you wouldn't need me today. Jenny was coming."

"I didn't need you to help. It's wading through this rain when you're not used to it."

She went to the kitchen, and a moment later she was back with towels over her shoulder and a steaming kettle in her hands. In front of the fireplace two chairs were drawn up; two pails set on newspapers.

"Oh, Mother, no!" I cried. "We've been in five houses today and I've had to soak my feet five times."

She was undisturbed. "Never mind. You can soak them again." She glanced up at Father, "You, too."

Without a word he put one foot on my footstool and begain unlacing his shoe. There was no use arguing when Mother gave an order. I took mine off, too. Mother went back to the kitchen with the kettle.

"Look at that," I said, holding up one foot. "I'll bet it's shrunk two sizes."

Father said, "Never seen such a mass footwashing since Grandma Clayborne's revival days. Now there was a good old Baptist." He gingerly touched one foot in his pail of water. "Scott! That's hot!" He whistled through his teeth.

"Doesn't faze me," I said. "I could stick pins in mine now and I wouldn't feel it."

Jenny came in with soup—big thick bowls full of a taste and aroma that had never been so good before. Soon, with the warmth inside us, and the crackling of the woodfire in the cozy room, the cold and tiredness of the day seemed long past. I stretched and yawned. "I feel an almighty lethargy coming on."

Father set his soup bowl on the floor and lifted his feet from the water. "I've had enough of this," he said.

"I'm too lazy to get up."

I leaned back in the chair and Father put on his dry socks and rubber houseshoes and clumped upstairs to Little Doc's room.

Mother was putting Melie Kate and Ruth to bed. I could hear Ruth arguing about how she got such a low mark in spelling the day before. When the dishes finished clattering in the kitchen, and later the back door slammed, I knew that Jenny had gone home. The house was warm and quiet.

I must have dozed there by the fire. Suddenly I sat up straight, wide awake and listening. Someone was coming up the path! It was a man's footsteps, quick and heavy—then a leap from the bottom step up to the porch.

"It's Bill!" I almost shouted. "Mother! Father! Bill's here!"

They couldn't have heard. The stairway door was closed.

Bill banged on the front door. "Hey! Anyone in there?"

"I'm here, Bill. Wait a minute!"

I started to rise—but my feet! I couldn't let Bill see me with my feet in a pail of water.

"Mother!" I called louder, but she couldn't hear. When the stairway door was shut, not a sound could be heard upstairs.

I grabbed the blanket on Father's chair and draped it across my lap and the water pail, and said "Come in, Bill—" but Bill was already in.

He grinned at me. "Hello, Spareribs."

I could only look at him. He hadn't changed a bit. Still tall and thin, still with the grin under the cowlick that never stayed back. He had looked that way when I had first seen him, when he had only been fourteen, hanging around Father's office after school, reading all the medical books in Father's bookcases, begging to straighten up the glass cases full of instruments, discussing plans with Little Doc to have their offices together some day. Six years in medical school, one summer in Budapest, now resident surgeon in St. Louis City Hospital, and the grin and the cowlick were still the same.

Only the clothes looked a bit different now. They were too well tailored, too well fitted.

"Well, Spareribs," he said again. "Rheumatism?"

I flushed. "I've put ten pounds on those ribs since you were last here," I said stiffly. "And it isn't rheumatism. It's gout."

He came over to stand by Father's chair. "A year since I've seen you and I find you so aged that you take the hot water cure for stiff joints. What do you do about crows' feet, Grandma?"

"I'm catching a cold," I said furiously. I could never be teased.

The door at the landing opened and Father came down. He took the five steps from the landing so fast that his rubbers nearly tripped him. Bill met him at the bottom.

"I got off earlier than I thought I could," Bill said. Then they couldn't seem to find much else to talk about. Father never could when Bill came back.

I waited, angry and embarrassed. The water grew colder and clammier. Finally, Father remembered Little Doc, and he and Bill went upstairs.

Quickly I dried my feet, put on my houseshoes, and carried the pails to the kitchen. Up the back stairs to my room, one look in the mirror and I groaned. No wonder Bill had laughed at me. No swamp girl had ever looked more bedraggled and windblown than I.

It was thirty minutes before I went downstairs again. My dress was changed and my hair was pinned up. Mother and Father and Bill were popping corn at the fireplace.

"Leverett's got more ideas than you can shake a stick at," Bill was saying. "He wraps that hospital around his finger."

I took my footstool from the corner and sat by Mother's chair.

"I remember Leverett," Father said. "We both taught courses at Tulane a couple of ten summers ago. We all understood then that he was a man of great weight." He held up the cornpopper and took a look inside. "Yes, sir, as my friend Washington Irving once said, 'In his own estimation he's a man of great weight—when he goes East, the West tips up.' "

Bill's laugh didn't ring all the way through. "He's been teaching me a lot about allergy," he said. "I think he's full of excellent ideas. He certainly makes enough money out of them."

Father shook the popper over the fire again. "I knew a doctor once whose front doorknob cost twenty dollars. He disappeared mysteriously . . . just gave one whoop and ran into the night. They put his doorknob on the poorhouse."

Something was wrong here. Father was too cryptic, Bill too defensive.

"Mary," Mother said. "There's doughnuts in the kitchen. How about it?"

"I'll get them."

Everything was right in the room when I returned. Bill's laugh was as I remembered. Father was telling him about Old Phineas Granther, at Mount Horeb back country, and the annual family reunion that was being held at his house the next day.

"Twelve children, thirty-nine grandchildren, twenty-six great grand-children," Father said. Bill whistled. "Old Phineas is a great man. Ought to see the politicians come shining up when it gets around election time. The Granthers are the voting majority in Ellis County. However Phineas goes, they all go—he's still boss." Father reached for the big bowl and poured the snow white popcorn in it. "In fact, if you'd like to, you might come out with me tomorrow. Thought I'd go out for a while. I delivered every one of those grandchildren."

"I'd like to go," Bill answered. "Strange I've never met him. Was he ever in the office?"

"Never was. He's the High Lama of the back country. The mountain goes to Mahomet, not Mahomet to the mountain."

I filled the popper for Father again, then sat back on my footstool. Mother wasn't saying much tonight. She sat quietly in her chair; none of her quick energy was around her. I didn't like to see her face so drawn and tired—her mouth without the quirk that always seemed secretly amused at something.

I reached up and put my hand on the arm of her chair. In a moment her hand closed over mine. We had sat this way once, late of an evening, when I had been a little girl and had asked her what music was.

"Oh, it's so many things," she had answered. "This is music—sitting here like this."

I hadn't understood. "You're not telling me, Mother! What is it?"

"Oh, it's when leaves turn red in autumn. It's when my little girl cries for the moon and I can't get it for her. It's when Ruthie bumps her head. It's when Melie Kate takes her doll and goes to sleep under a tree out in the woods and I get frightened, thinking she's lost."

I had been too young. "Oh, Mother!"

"It's when Robert is home in the evening, and we sit here in front of the fire, knowing our children are asleep and safe upstairs." She wasn't talking to me any more. "It's when Little Doc would work all day long making a kite, and then it would be top-heavy and wouldn't fly, and he would say, 'The next one will fly, Mother—next time it will fly'—that's music . . ."

I could still see her face with the strong profile, the glow of the fire on her black hair. I could still hear her voice.

Yes, and it was when dear friends sat together, as we four sat now, and no words were needed. We had sat there for a long moment, no one speaking.

Father turned to me. "Give us a tune, Sissie."

How many times he had put my thoughts into words! I wanted to play tonight. There was so much to be happy for. The day had been so rich, now the evening so full. I played for that feeling in the room.

Later, something made me look up from the keys. Bill was standing by the mantelpiece, his hands in his pockets. There was no grin. His eyes were dark. In that instant I knew that he had been watching me for a long time.

Something swept over me from head to foot, and I looked down at the keys again—but the thread was broken. I was finished playing. The day was done and I wanted to go to my room.

I avoided Bill's eyes when I want back to the fireplace and kissed Mother and Father goodnight. Then I had to look at him.

"Goodnight, Bill."

"Goodnight, Mary."

I walked over to the stairway, up the stairs, along the hall to my room. Without the light on, I sat at my window and looked out through the branches of the sweet-gum tree, to the streetlight shining hazily through the mists. Something was changing for me—I had felt it again tonight. It had been in Bill's eyes, and his voice when he called me "Mary," for the first time since I had known him.

# III

THE SUN, HOT on my face, awakened me the next morning. It came through my open window, bringing the smell of damp earth and clean washed air. It was Easter. The trees had buds.

"Sister," Mother called up the stairs. "Listen out your window—wild ducks."

I lay still—a faint, distant crackling came from the clouds. Yes, it was spring.

I jumped from bed and grabbed my clothes from the chair. Someone was whistling outside. Bill was coming down the road from Maple Street, his hands in his pockets, his cowlick standing straight up.

As I stood there, watching him come past the big oak tree, into the yard, remembrance of the evening before came back to me. It had been such a strange, disturbing feeling for Bill to bring—he had been a friend since my pigtail days.

He glanced up toward my window, still whistling. I didn't move—he couldn't see me through the screen of branches. But he called, "Hi, Spareribs! Hurry down—it's church time."

"It's only eight-thirty," I called back—but the feeling had gone with the sound of his voice. This was still Bill. The evening before must have been my imagination. It must have been the mood of the fire, the music, the happiness in the house because he was back again. Yes, of course that was it. I hurried to the closet for my new blue dress, and combed my hair to go down to breakfast.

After church, Father and Bill and I set out for Mount Horeb. It was an hour's drive, twelve miles out on the Tom Box road.

The day was perfect for Easter. The earth was a rich dark brown. Ships with sails rode through the sky.

I laughed. "Even the elements know enough to behave when Old Phineas has a family reunion."

"Mind you step like you got a briar in your heel, too," Father answered. "Something's up. Old Phineas asked for you today."

"Probably because Little Doc couldn't come."

Bill said, "Probably because he had so many young grandsons that he figures one of them might serve to get their doctoring free."

Father chuckled, but I didn't laugh. I didn't like to be teased about marriage.

The car turned onto a side road that was a serpent from Hawthorne's tales, undulating its length over five small hills leading to Phineas Granther's white house on the crest of the last hill.

"I wish you would look," I said. "There's kinfolks all over the place. Looks like an ant hill."

From where we were on the first mound, the figures on the last hill were tiny and indistinct, sitting on the porch, standing by the pillars, climbing the hill from the orchard, even smaller figures running in the yard. We had topped the third mound before I spotted Old Phineas in his high cane chair on the front porch, a patriarch among his tents. Then we were climbing the steep road that led to the house, and the figures on the porch were standing, waiting for us.

Old Phineas stood from his chair when we came up.

"Sit down, old man," Father said, "I stand with your children today." His voice was so warm that it tingled on the back of my neck.

"Children, grandchildren, and great-grandchildren today," Phineas answered.

He held out his gnarled hand to Father. His gray eyes were shining beads in his sallow, wrinkled face. What had Father called him? High Lama, yes.

The gray eyes turned to me.

"This is Mary," Father said.

The knotty hand stretched toward mine. The beady eyes seemed to bore through me. "Ye're Big Doc's gal, all right," he said.

Father motioned toward Bill. "This is Dr. Sheehan. I've told you about him. He'll be driving his car in place of mine some day."

A hundred pair of eyes turned toward Bill. A hundred minds seemed to pick up my thoughts and carry them ahead with theirs. Big Doc gives them his successor? No one is given to the back country. They take it first. Didn't Big Doc know that?

Old Phineas shook Bill's hand and smiled a thousand wrinkles more. "We welcome ye, Doctor."

The eyes turned back again. Old Phineas would decide.

Dinner was spread in the orchard. Long tables were set out under the trees; one for the children, another for the grandchildren, still another for the great-grandchildren. There were children everywhere—yelling and laughing and screaming. Babies crawled underfoot.

Father spoke to a young girl with a baby on her hip. "When you aim to wean that youngest of yours, Jess? Seems to me he's old enough to walk."

"He's walkin' all right," she answered. "I'll git to weanin' him soon as the signs git right. Might be right now fer all I know. Our almanac blowed out the winder oncet and Earl ain't never got another'n."

Father said, "Well, you get another one and see about it. He should be feeding himself by now."

"She's gittin' pore as a winter chicken, too," a woman said, who stood by Jess. "She ain't nothin' but a shadder—waddlin' around all the time with thet big young'un astraddle 'er hip."

"She's the best-looking gal in Ellis County," Father answered. "Got the smartest boy, too."

The first woman blushed. The second tipped her head back and shrilled with laughter. "I'm goin' to tell Miz Doc on you, Doctor Clayborne. You've done told thet to every woman back h'year."

Father laughed his short dry laugh. "You're still the best-lookin' gal in Jed Granther's house, Omie."

The woman shrieked again. "Listen to him will ye? I got five big knots of boys and he says I'm the best-lookin' gal in the house." She shook her finger at him. "I'm the sorriest-lookin' one, too, Big Doc!"

"Tut, tut, Omie," he said.

We walked on down the path between the trees. Phineas' back was bent and he leaned on his cane, but his spry steps covered the ground as quickly as Father and Bill's long strides did.

A chubby baby scuttled across in front of us, crawling over to one of the women working at a table. He clutched her skirt and pulled himself to his feet, wobbly and uncertain. She turned from her work and looked down on him. "Dearest lamb," she said, her face tender and soft. "Mother's lamb." he stood, unsteady and fat, laughing up at her. Only a moment—then he chuckled and gurgled and sat down hard. The woman turned back to the table. "Hey, thar, Gert," she called shrilly to a girl a table away. "Git in the kitchen and git thet coffeepot. Hit's perkin' its guts out by now." The baby crawled on. The woman picked up her basket and stepped over him on her way to another table.

Bill's voice speaking to Old Phineas brought me back. "How many acres do you have here, Mr. Granther?"

"Two hundred and ten," Phineas answered amiably.

Bill whistled softly. "How many cultivated?"

Phineas hesitated only a fraction of a second. "About eighty-five's cultivated."

"What a pile of money a man could make from this ground. It's black as the ace of spades. Look at that hill over yonder—what a vineyard it would make!" Bill was excited. Phineas said nothing. "And think what a dairy farm there could be in the valley there. And the timber! Look at that one!" He pointed far up the hill to a tall pine, towering and majestic, hundreds of years old. "A lumber mill would give you a fortune for that tree. There wouldn't be a knothole in a thirty-foot plank."

Phineas looked out over the valley. "Ah, yes," he said, musing.

Then he leaned on his cane and turned toward the tables again. Father strode beside him.

Phineas leaned his cane against an apple tree when he reached his chair, and he stood until all the tables were seated. Father sat at Phineas' right. Bill and I were on the left, midway down the table.

Heads bowed, and Old Phineas stood there, his gnarled old hands leaning on the table, his wrinkled face erect and looking out over his children. "Our Kind Father," he said. "For our days of fullness we thank Thee. For the needs of our bodies, and Thy measure of earth that providest them, we are thankful. Amen."

An hour later we walked back up the path, to the porch. Old Phineas sat in his high cane chair. "Git some cheers, Otho," he said to a boy standing by the door. "Git a rocker fer Miss Mary."

"No chair for me," Father said. He sat on the top step and leaned his back against the porch pillar. When the rocking-chair came, Bill pulled up one of the straight chairs and sat next to me.

The children were running in the yard again. Down the hill, by the potato patch, two of the older boys were fighting. Six younger cousins stood around, cheering and yelling.

"Them two allus gits in a fight when they meet," the boy by the door said.

"Go stop them, Otho," Phineas said.

Otho ran down the steps and out toward the scuffling, shouting group. Father crossed his hands behind his head and looked after him. "Behold, how good and how pleasant it is for cousins to dwell together in unity," he quoted. "It is like the precious oil upon the head." Old Phineas chuckled with Father.

"How many more did we get this year, Phineas?" Father asked.

"Eight more. Five girls, three boys. Come Thanksgivin' and ye'll be bringin' my first great-great-grandson."

"Esther's girl?"

"Jed's grandson. Buford. Married Christmas."

Father laughed. "I remember. Jed swallowed three cuds of 'Star Navy' and I had to sit up with him all night. He was more scared than the boy."

The group had quieted down, by the potato patch, and Father and Old Phineas looked out over the yard full of children.

"You can feel as proud as Old Father Abraham with that spawn, Phineas," Father said. "Not a bad one in the lot."

Old Phineas leaned forward and rested his chin on the knotty hands that curved over the handle of the cane. "I ain't got no edication," he said simply.

Father was silent for a moment. Then he stretched his long legs out on the porch before him, and leaned back against the pillar again. "Yes, sir, here we sit. Solomon and Methuselah. The Student Everlasting, the Ancient of Days." He chuckled to himself. "Solomon got to go to school and get wise, but Methuselah had to stay home and cut hay. Still, I'll bet that when Solomon went around to stay till bedtime and eat popcorn, that he sat in the corner on the woodbox and said nothing. Or, if he started off on something like, 'Behold thou art fair, my Love, behold thou art fair, thou hast dove's eyes,' that Methuselah would take a fresh chew of tobaccy and say, 'Yes, but Sol, you ought to have seen her great-grandmother's eyes.' 'But what do you know about her?' 'Took her to a candy pulling down on the River Jordan four hundred and sixty-nine years ago.'"

Old Phineas chuckled until his head bobbed up and down. Father laughed with him. They were two alone on the porch. The feeling that I had felt on the fence that night, welled up in my throat again. What was my Father, that he was one of these people, speech of these people, yet so alone and so far apart?

My thought was broken by the man who sat next to me, on my left. He was a tall, gaunt, black-bearded man. His chair had been leaning back, propped against the wall of the house. Now it came down on all four legs, and the man leaned forward with his elbows balanced on his knees. He took a sack of tobacco and a packet of cigarette papers from his shirt pocket.

"I hear tell you play the orgin," he said to me, still looking down at the tobacco sack.

"I play the piano," I answered. "There's not much difference if it's a foot organ."

He carefully poured the tobacco in the thin paper. "I live out to Granite Hill," he said.

This was Jake Granther, then. Old Phineas's sixth son, the beloved Reuben of his house.

"We aim to git an orgin out to the church house soon," he said. "We ain't got no one to play, howsomever."

What was he trying to ask me? He pulled the string of the tobacco sack and put it back in his shirt pocket. I didn't know what to answer, and he was waiting.

"Mary's still in school," Father said. "Figures she has to finish learning how to add two and two before she can show someone how to push four keys down all at once."

That was it! This man was asking me to come out and teach them when they got their new organ.

Jake Granther's big hands were cupped around his cigarette, and smoke puffed out. "Be a year or two afore we git it," he said.

"Oh, thank you," I said. "I do plan to be a teacher some day."

He nodded and flipped the match into the yard. Then he leaned his chair back against the wall and looked out over the yard. He had had his say.

I couldn't see Father's face, but I knew the pride he was feeling from Jake Granther's words. Ah, yes, he would be proud, but how could I tell this big man who had so honored me, that my plans lay far beyond the back country? Next autumn, when Jed's grandson would listen to his son's first cry, I would be far away in the Conservatory, meeting the people I had always wanted to meet, practicing the hours that I had been waiting for, hearing the music that I was so hungry to hear. My plans were far from the back country.

Bill spoke low by my ear. "Come out of the fog, Spareribs. Come on back."

I laughed. "I wasn't very far away."

"I know exactly where you were," he said, and suddenly I knew that he did.

We left that evening as the cowbells were tinkling at the pasture gate. Driving home, Bill said, "About that girl with the child, in the orchard this afternoon. Why do you keep on letting them wean their children by almanacs, the same as they plant their beans? Why don't you educate them?"

Father said, "I sometimes deplore the fact that the word 'education' was ever put in the English language."

Bill's finger tapped nervously on the car door. "I sometimes deplore the fact that I've been with you for ten years, and I still don't know what it is that you get out of a lot of this. About half of it would do for me. There must be something in it if there's not money. What do you get?"

"Just a living, Bill. Just a living."

Bill laughed and shook his head. "That's the word I wish I had the definition for," he said. "Never means the same thing twice."

Father had no answer.

# IV

BILL HAD TO leave on the 10:30 train, Monday night. He had been given only three days leave from the hospital.

In the afternoon, Monday, he came to bring Little Doc a chart of the nervous system. Little Doc was out of bed: he and Bill sat in the living-room and discussed blood pressures and appendectomies. I was sitting on the stairsteps with Melie Kate. Her doll had suddenly gone cross-eyed, and it was my job to take off its scalp and do an operation with a big needle.

"I think I'll do my first appendectomy on Sister," Little Doc said. "It takes a pal for that."

"I'm not that good a pal," I said. "You can pick on Bill for that mark of friendship."

Bill reached over and turned Little Doc's hand palm up. "You'll be a surgeon, all right," he said. "It's written right there." We had always known that. Little Doc's hand were like Father's—long and lean and sensitive, yet, contradictorily, awkward and ungainly.

"Only one more year of school after this one, then I start Pre-Med," Little Doc said.

"Where to?"

Little Doc's voice was surprised. "The University." Both Father and Bill had gone there.

"Footprints in the sands of time, Little Doc," Bill laughed. "I was 'Third Seat Back Row' to Professor Hotchins for four semesters."

He stood up, and ran his hand through his hair. The cowlick stood on end. "Hey, there, Spareribs," he said. "If I go home and saddle Sam and Sooky, could we take a ride down to Job's Landing and back?"

I looked up from the doll's cranial cavity. "I'd love to, Bill." None of us had been down to Job's Landing, in Black Hollow, for all of three years. We used to go fishing there.

"I'd like to see the old place," Bill said. "Some catfish we used to get there."

"There's worms in a can in the garage if you want to fish," Little Doc told him.

"No time for fishing today," Bill said.

The needle slipped and the eyes slid back where they had been again.

What was wrong with me that my imagination heard words unspoken? Of course there was no time for fishing—it was already the middle of the afternoon, and it was a long trip down to Job's Landing and back before supper.

I had almost fogotten how easy Sooky was to ride. Sam was getting old—he lumbered along with Bill, but Sooky was as swift and light as ever.

Nonetheless, Bill beat me to Job's Landing. He pulled Sam up to the old shack by the swamp, and dismounted to wait for me.

"Give Sooky a rest and let's see if old Three-Pipes is still here," he said, when I came up.

I jumped off Sooky before Bill could help me down. "He's not here, Bill. He went to Oklahoma two winters ago. I thought I told you."

Bill looked at the sagging old shack, the iron-chained door, the barred windows. He put his hands in his pockets and leaned back on his heels. "Three-Pipes Job," he laughed. " 'You kin fish fer five cents as long as hit takes me to smoke me pipe three times,' he'd say. I wonder what he thought we'd catch in this old place except catfish, anyway."

I stood beside him on the pier. There was an eerie fascination in the scene before us. The stagnant water was green and turgid. The trunks of the willows were swollen far up their trunks, the tall grasses and cattails waved in the wind. I stopped down and picked a sprig of redbud to take Mother.

"Say," Bill exclaimed. "I thought this place was supposed to be drained a year or so ago."

"It was drained. Now it's a backwash."

"From what?"

I pointed to the long, low hill behind us. "Newcastle Hill," I said. "It's been made into a snitzy residential section. They built three big lakes for the water supply, because it's too far away from the river to pump water easily, and some way the backwash gets down here."

"Perfect place for anopheles to bring up their families."

"I know. Look at them."

The surface of the thick water quivered with insects that lived below. Dragonflies swooped down and around. "I love it here as well as the mosquitoes do," I said. Bill shuddered.

We sat on the pier and dangled our feet over the water. The soles of our boots made four long wavering shadows.

"Big feet you've got there, Grandma," Bill observed.

"These aren't my boots. They're Little Doc's. You don't think that I can still wear the boots that I had when you left for school? That was seven years ago."

"Seven years ago." Bill was speaking to my shadow in the water. "I remember what you said when the train pulled out. You said, 'I'm going too, some day,' and I said, 'Come on, we'll go together,' and you said, 'It's not time for me yet.' That was a funny thing for a girl still in bloomer dresses to say."

"I don't remember saying it," I said.

"You probably remember that that was the summer that I spent more time on Mimi Abbott's front porch than I did on yours."

"I was furious, Bill. We thought you were going to marry her." I leaned over and peered at my face in the water. "Look how I'd look if I were jelly," I said.

Bill ignored it. "You always got angry at me for nothing. I had told you for years that I was waiting for you to grow up."

"You did not. You always said that spareribs and sauerkraut just naturally go together. You were trying to be funny."

"When you're seventeen I'll consider you grown up. Then I'll ask you to marry me."

"I'm seventeen next month." I threw a small pebble in the water, and my face grew wide and grinning like a pumpkin.

"Then I'll ask you," Bill said. "What will you say?"

"Oh, I don't know. Probably that you're much too old for me."

"Ten years older. Big Doc's twenty years older than your mother. That doesn't matter. I've loved you since you broke your tennis racket over my head. Farther back than that—since I could carry you around by your overall straps." Bill's voice wasn't right. The conversation had gone off on a tangent somewhere. "I've tried to hurry you into growing up. I brought you your first lipstick, remember?"

The face in the water below was bobbing its head sadly now. "It wasn't the right color," I said. "Mother wouldn't let me wear it."

Bill's hands were on my shoulders and he turned me to face him. "Mary, I don't believe you understood me. I'm saying 'I love you very much. I've always loved you. I want you to marry me some day.' I don't know a new way of saying it."

Bill had never looked like this before. His eyes, his mouth, his hands on my shoulders—he had never been serious before. Always the grin.

"I—Bill, I'm only sixteen." I didn't know what to say to him. "I've not thought about marrying anyone yet."

He grinned—but a grin that I had never seen before. "You don't have to think about it yet. I haven't asked you yet. This is a sort of Prelude. I can't be here on your seventeenth birthday—I'm telling you now so you'll know what I'm talking about when I write to you."

I looked down and turned away from him. "You've always been my friend, Bill—"

"I still am. Until you're seventeen." When I didn't answer, he laughed and turned me to face him again. "Hey, wait a minute, Chicken Little. The sky hasn't fallen in."

His smile faded as he looked at me. One hand left my shoulder and came slowly toward my face. Another second and he had slapped me, sharply, hard.

"Bill!"

"Mosquitoes," he said noncommittally. "Three of them. Big enough to roast."

He got to his feet and pulled me to mine. "Get your tree, Spareribs, and let's go. It's late."

I watched him walk back to Three-Pipes' shack and untie Sooky and Sam. He turned and grinned at me. Then I picked up the sprig of redbud and we left the pier and Job's Landing.

When we reached home, I went straight to the kitchen where Father was. He stood by the kitchen table, shaking down his thermometer.

"Who is sick now?" I asked. "Still Little Doc?"

"Mother," he answered.

"Bill has to leave now. He's in the living-room."

Father slipped the thermometer back in its case and put it in his inside coat pocket. He went into the living-room, his hand outstretched for Bill's. "It was good to see you again, Son. Get yourself back soon."

Bill's hand gripped Father's, hard. "The next day I get off will mark the beginning of the long, long row to hoe."

"I'll have the shovels waiting," Father answered.

Was it my imagination, or did Bill hesitate a bit too long to answer? "Only four months to go," he said, and there was no clue either way in his voice.

He picked up his hat from the table and jammed it on his head. "Go find your brethren, Spareribs," he said to me. "I have farewells to make. Where's Miz Doc?" he asked Father.

"In bed with flu," Father answered. "I'll give her your goodbye."

I went outside to find Melie Kate and Ruth and Little Doc. Bill had left Job's Landing far behind. No trace of it had crossed the threshold of the house.

# V

MOTHER WAS IN bed for two weeks. When Easter vacation was over and school began again, Jenny came to stay all day. It was strange to come home to no piano lessons after school.

It was many a month after that before I listened to another lesson from behind the banister posts. When Mother was up at last, and sat white-faced and thin before the fire, Father was firm. "No more teaching this year. Not until school starts again."

"Oh, no, Robert!" Mother was just as firm. "I can't leave my pupils near the end of the season like this. Jim Ellis is to play the piano solo for commencement. Martha is just in again after being ill—oh, no. Wait until school is out."

A few evenings later, Dr. White "dropped in." He and Father had begun practicing in the same office, twenty years before. When Dr. White stood up to leave, he galumphed in his beard, stuck his stomach out and said exactly what Father had.

"This isn't just flu, Mrs. Clayborne. It's overwork, malaria and a little bit of a whole lot."

Mother sniffed. Dr. White galumphed even louder. "No more teaching until September," he said, much firmer than Father had, then turned and went out the front door before Mother exploded.

So the piano stool stood empty after school now. Melie Kate and Ruth and I were Mother's only pupils.

There was no word from Bill in the weeks that passed. For a while I had almost been afraid to come home from school and look through the mail on the dining-room table—if Bill had written, there would have been teasing, and his words had opened a door for me that was still too new and insecure to take teasing. Too many hitherto vague thoughts had suddenly been set in bold relief.

Oddly, the one which loomed largest, huge and devouring, was the dream that had always been with me. I wanted to be a piano teacher. I had always planned to leave for the Conservatory as soon as high school was finished. There had never been a doubt in my mind. It was written so. I had always known it.

Father and I talked about it one evening in late May, sitting on the front-porch swing after supper.

I leaned against his shoulder, my feet up in the swing before me. The air was clean and cool, with a soft night wind blowing. The sky was dotted with stars; the milky way over the oak tree, the Big Dipper in the open space between the porch pillars.

"Father, when I register at the Conservatory, I think I'll leave out my middle name. 'Mary' is enough."

"What's the matter with 'Myrtle'?"

"Oh—people make fun of it."

"That's your Mother's name."

"Yes, and it's Myrtle Jetson's, too. Myrtle's awful. She's coarse and dirty, she wears bells on her garters—she's the one who hopped a freight train in the freight yard that time and was caught in Kansas City."

"I remember Myrtle."

"I've never dared tell anybody in school what my middle name is. I'd never hear the end of it."

Father started the swing moving with his foot. He said, "I named you Myrtle because it was cool and dark and fragrant. It's like spring, and you were born in May." To hear Father speak, "Myrtle" was a name that belonged with the soft night wind and the silver stars. "Anyway, it was your Mother's name," he said again.

The swing creaked in the cool still air. Back and forth, back and forth, Father's foot keeping it in slow motion.

"I know why Mother named me Mary," I said, later. "She said that when I was first born, she took one look at me and decided that 'Mary' was the safest name she could think of. She said it would fit anything from a Queen of Scotland to Bloody Mary Malone in Black Hollow."

Father chuckled. His chin touched the top of my head. "Bill tells me that he went courting in Black Hollow a while back," he said.

A tingling went down to my fingertips. There was a moment that grew close and waiting around us.

"Do you love him, Sister?"

I waited for the answer. "No, sir," I said. Something relaxed in me.

"Need any help?" His voice was matter-of-fact. I felt the hard shoulder behind me, his big rough hand over mine. I would always know how to make my decisions—Father would always be just behind me.

"Not yet," I answered.

The swing creaked on. The wind must have been blowing the stars, too; they twinkled and wavered. There was the feeling again that I had felt on the steps one March day. This was all part of a pattern. No matter what I said or thought, something was happening that I was a part of—no word of mine could stop it. There was a heavy pain in my throat.

"I don't know what it means to love someone enough to marry him," I said to Father. "The only kind of love that I've seen is the kind that you and Mother have, and that's not the kind that I feel for Bill. I don't seem to have any feeling for Bill. Except as he always was—just Bill."

"Don't worry about it, Sissie. You'll know when you've found the right one."

"It's not time for him yet, Father." If only the pain would leave my throat. "There's so much that I have to do first. I want to be a piano teacher."

Father didn't answer.

"I want to do what Mother does. She can take someone like Rickie Powers—a half-wit—and make music come out of his hands. I can feel her shaping a lesson—molding a lesson. It's beautiful, Father."

"That's something else, little girl."

"That's teaching?" It came out a question.

"That's touching something here," he touched my chest, "not here," pointing to my hands. "You don't learn that in a conservatory."

"Oh, but I can make myself the best I can be," I said, eagerly. The pain was almost gone now. "Mother did that. Grandfather did that. Aunt Melie and Uncle Webbie teach the same way. They all studied years and years first. I want to study the way you did, too. I don't want to be mediocre. I want to be the best that I am."

"We have to learn to be mediocre to be the best that we are," he answered.

"Oh, Father!"

"Emerson called it moderation," he said. "The Preacher sayeth, 'Vanity of vanities, all is vanity.' The Chinese call it half-and-half. Lincoln called it 'the common man'—"

"Oh, Father! Stop it!" I sat up angrily and turned to face him. "You're making fun of me." I was close to tears.

His hands were iron and they turned me back to look at the sky again. "I'll show you a star. See there?" His bony finger pointed. Arcturus shone clear and bright in the heavens. "There's billions of stars up there, but you can have only one."

"I only want one."

"Sometimes, there are people born with the star already burning inside them. They don't have to go searching for it; it brought them here in the first place." His hand was heavy on mine. "Those people are born on a path, with their hands on someone's shoulder, and someone coming behind them with a hand on theirs. Their eyes are up there as straight as my finger can point. Everything they hear, everything they read, all points the same way. Nothing stops them. They don't see crevices, they walk through storms, they step on thorns—nothing matters. Their eyes are too far ahead of them." He hesitated. His voice came from all around me. "Only some of them forget to look around. It hurts to look around. You see paths and fields and woods. You see a smile that you had never had time to see to the end before. You see love that you took and hurried on with because there wasn't time to tarry. You hear songs that you forgot to sing—words that you forgot to say. You see that your footsteps are treading on blood and chains of the ones who were born loving you—"

Suddenly the swing stopped with a jolt. "Let's go in," Father said, short and brusque. He got up and strode to the door. "Come on, Sister. It's cold out here."

The screen door slammed behind him, and his rubbers clumped across the floor. Arcturus shone impassively as before. A wind came and pushed the swing, but there was no one behind me. It was cold.

# VI

IT WAS ALMOST a week before Father had another evening at home.

We sat in the living-room after supper—Mother, Father, Melie Kate, Ruth and I. Little Doc was in his room stuffing an owl. Father had started him on taxidermy.

Father sat back in his chair and crossed his hands behind his head. "A penny to the one who finds it," he said.

Melie and Ruth looked up from their schoolbooks.

"Finds what?"

"The penny!"

They scrambled to their feet and looked around frantically. "Under your shoes," Ruthie said, trying to move Father's feet. He held his feet up: his shadow made a gaunt spider on the ceiling. "Nope, no penny." He set them down again.

"Mother's got it!" Melie Kate was at her chair, pulling at her darning.

"No, no!" Mother said sharply. She was so impatient lately.

"It's not there, Melie Kate," Father said. "Look again."

There was a loud crash and Ruthie was on the floor, the rocking-chair on top of her.

"For Heaven's sakes, what did you do?" Mother asked.

"I wanted to look on the mantel," Ruth said through her tears.

"I've told you time and again not to stand in a rocking-chair. Come here, let me look at it." Ruthie got up and walked over to Mother, a big blue bump already coming on her forehead.

"Mother," Little Doc asked from the landing. "You know those old fox furs of yours in the attic? Can I have the eyes out of them for my owl?"

"Anything. Just keep it out of my sight."

"Thanks." He sped up the stairs again. Three bounds and he was at the top—a slam of a door and he was on his way to the attic.

"Time to go to bed," Mother said to Melie Kate and Ruth. "No Br'er Rabbit story tonight. It's too late."

"My reading's not done," Ruthie said.

"You can do it tomorrow while I'm getting breakfast." She wound her darning up and set the basket down by the side of her chair. "Say your prayers and we'll go."

"We didn't find the penny," Melie Kate reminded her.

"Prayers first," Father said. He looked across at me, his eyes mischievous.

The two girls knelt at Mother's knees. After a moment of indistinguishable mumbling they were up and then kneeling at Father's knees. His bony hands were on their bent heads.

Suddenly Melie Kate shrieked, "I've got it! I've got it!" "It's mine!" Ruth shrilled. "Get away, Melie Kate!" They dived for the penny under Father's chair, and he had to haul them out by their dress tails. "There's two of them," he said. "Just wait a minute."

Mother was on her way upstairs. "Devout little heathens," she remarked caustically to Father. He only grinned. But I could have sworn that for a moment his ears were pointed, and his hair came to a peak above his forehead.

After they left, Father reached up on the mantel and took down the big red apple that he had brought home for Mother. He flipped open his pocket-knife and began slowly peeling it.

"I think I'll go up to my room to finish studying," I said. "I'm almost finished. I'll just keep you and Mother from talking if I stay down here."

"When are examinations?"

"Next week. I'm still worried about trigonometry."

"Don't know why you worry." His voice was dry. "You've always known four months in advance what your final grade is going to be. You've flunked it every term since you started Clendenin."

"That's enough, now."

I gathered up my books and went over to the fireplace to kiss him goodnight. He cut off the apple peeling with a final flick and held the long scarlet curl up to me. "A corkscrew," he said, "to drill some reality into my dreamer's noggin."

"Yes, sir," I said.

A half-hour later I was done with studying. I was ready for bed, but it was too early to go to sleep yet. The book that I wanted, Beethoven's *Sketchbook* was in the bookcase at the foot of the stairs. I could tiptoe down and back in my bare feet and not bother Mother and Father.

One step before I reached the landing, I stopped short, I had heard the word "Conservatory." Father and Mother were discussing it! Excitement ran over me like a chill, and I ducked low behind the banisters and slid down to my old place on the fourth step. I had to hear this! I had waited too many years not to know the moment it was decided when I was to leave, and from whom I was to study.

The shadow was deep at the staircase. There was only the firelight in the long room. Father's back was half-turned toward me, Mother was in profile, her hands resting quietly on the arms of her chair. She never had mending there when she sat alone with Father.

"I wish children never had to be educated," she said. "Once Sister leaves, she'll never come back. I'm not afraid for Little Doc—he knows what he wants."

"Sister wants a dream, Myrtle," Father answered. "She'll be all right."

"Sister's always wanted a dream—but, Robert, I'm so afraid for her when she finds out that a dream isn't something that she can hold out her hand and receive."

Father sat forward, his elbows leaning on his knees. "She has to learn about it some time." He laughed—his short, brusque laugh. "Better wait and see if we can even give them the push out the door." Mother turned to look at him. "Four degrees of my own," he said, "and I haven't got a penny to send my son and daughter after one of theirs."

Mother's face turned back. "We'll find it when the time comes." Her voice seemed part of the quiet flicker of the flames.

Father shook his head. "Maybe we could manage for one. We can't for four. Sister is ready to leave next fall—Little Doc the next fall. Seven years for Little Doc. Seven years—" His voice trailed off.

Oh, Father, I saw what you saw then. This was Big Doc, tall and straight and strong. The clipped iron-gray mustache, the long swinging stride. But his hair was gray, there were sixty-five years on the calendar— seven years more to go, and then two other little girls coming after—what were seven years more on sixty-five? Suddenly it was an old, old man, sitting there leaning toward the fire, his back tired, his gaunt hands gnarled and veined with age.

Then, just as suddenly, the apparition was gone, and Father straightened in his chair. "I have something for you," he said to Mother. "Came a couple of days ago." He took an envelope from the pocket of his coat and handed it across to Mother.

Mother turned to the side a little, to read by the light of the fire. The flames crackled nervously: the wind rattled at the window.

She folded the letter and put it back in the envelope. "Do you want to leave here?" she asked Father.

"I think so." He leaned forward again, and chuckled. "Might be nice having the young men about town saying, 'See the old codger in the purple shirt, there? Dr. Clayborne, New Dean of Medical Research at Missouri State. His wife pours tea with her little finger in the air.' "

"We'd all have to tear up roots," Mother said.

Father pointed to the letter. "There's roots there for their future, though. There's an excellent medical school for Little Doc in the same city. It means the Conservatory for Mary, art school for Melie Kate later—" He chuckled dryly. "Enough salary to keep Ruthie in Mercurochrome for the rest of her life."

Mother's mouth quirked. She handed the letter back to Father. "I don't believe we want it, Robert," she said.

I was stunned. Father must have been, too; his hand remained out-stretched, the letter in it. "You don't understand, Myrtle. They're offering me Dean of Research."

"I read it."

He stuffed the letter in his pocket. "Look here, Myrtle, you're holding on to something not worth holding on to. We don't belong here. None of us do. We're not in the town, we're not in the country—we don't speak any language. This gives us everything we want. It pays in greenbacks, not turnips."

I had never heard these words before—this voice.

"I'm sorry, Robert," Mother said. "I won't go."

"Well, we'll have to go." His voice was edged. "It's the way to do it."

They sat silent in their chairs. Mother's hands gripped the arms of her chair. The fire sputtered futilely; the wind moaned around the house.

Finally Father spoke. His voice was flat. "There's nothing to stay here for, Myrtle. I haven't done anything that we came here to do. It's not been worth a continental—the people in the town still laugh at us."

"Once you didn't care," Mother said.

"Once I didn't know that living on a hill was as much a dream as Sister's wanting to get to her school. I thought all we had to do was to get here—the rest would take care of itself." He looked down at his hands. "One Sunday Melie Kate and I were walking down on the sandbar by the river, and I said, 'Walk behind, Melie. Follow in my footsteps.' She looked down at the tracks and said, 'But Father, you don't make many.' " His laugh seared through me.

Mother didn't turn. "Once, a long time ago, you came to this hill to fight malaria. What happened to that?"

"Where have I taken them? Twenty years against ignorance and superstition, and they still pour the quinine down the creek. They still won't send for me until they're black with fever. They lie about it. All they want me for is to dig out their bullets and deliver their children."

"Ah, how you've failed, Robert," Mother said.

"I'm done with it here."

Her words were ice. "You've failed because you've never fought. You haven't fought for anything." The firelight cut her face into lines of granite. "You came to a hill to fight, and instead you've buried your head in your books and your dreams."

He looked at her. Her face was immovable.

"I've given everything I had to give, Myrtle," he said.

"You've given everything you could give without picking up a bean-shooter and going down in the valley to fight."

Father didn't answer.

Mother leaned toward him. "Why don't you fight FOR something for a change, Robert—not always against something? If your people back country don't know how to get what they need, why don't you get it for them? They don't know how to fight for themselves. They don't know anything about politics—they don't know what to ask for or who to talk to. Who would understand them if they did? Look, Robert—" How eager her voice was. "Why don't you get rid of their mosquitoes, instead of just fighting the malaria? Why don't you get their marshes drained and their swamps cut down? Dosing them with quinine isn't the way. You told me a moment ago that we didn't speak the language of either the town or the country, but the thing is that you speak both—you could do it! You hold a great power in your hands—I know you do!"

"I'm no politician," he said sharply.

She sat back in her chair again. "No, you only want to sit in your chapel and look up at your stained-glass windows." Her voice was almost trembling with anger. "I won't go with you to be a dean's wife, Robert. I didn't start walking that way."

They sat unmoving, the air split between them. In the fireplace a log fell through soundlessly: the flames danced silently. Outside, the wind tiptoed around the corner.

Then, shatteringly, someone knocked at the side door.

My heart pounded. Mother's grip loosened on the chair arm. Father strode to the dining-room door, opened it, and went on to the side door. The bolt caught and he wrenched the door open. "Yes?" His voice was harsh.

"Big Doc—I—"

The voices were lost in the night wind.

His footsteps were quieter when he returned. He crossed to his chair and took his rubber houseshoes off. "Where are my shoes?" he asked.

Mother still looked at the fire. "Melie Kate shined them. They must be in the kitchen." Her voice was matter-of-fact, everyday, part of the knock at the door.

Father rose and walked in his stocking feet to the closet under the stairs. "Won't be back until morning," he said, shrugging into his coat. "Maternity case."

He took his medicine case from the bookcase. "Better come bolt the door after me."

At the dining-room door he turned and came back to Mother. "Goodnight," he said. He touched her on the forehead.

"Goodnight, Robert." Her hand came up and pulled his head down to hers. Only an instant, then he straightened again.

He turned, and was gone. A moment later the side door closed and his footsteps went down the path to the wagon.

Mother sat there, her face immobile in the firelight. Her profile was graven: something glistened on her cheek. The little flames danced and talked to her. The wind ran around the house, angrily complaining because the doors and windows were closed to him. He had to be content to whisper to her through the casement cracks.

# VII

FATHER CAME IN a little before breakfast the next morning. His face was gray and tired, his mouth hurt at the corners.

"Don't ask anything about it," Mother told us in the kitchen. "The woman died."

All the way to school that morning, all during the day, words hammered and pounded in my head. It was my seventeenth birthday, and the sun was shining—but all that I could hear were words that I had heard the evening before. Everything said the same—Trigonometry, History, Economics—

After school was out, I waited at the steps for Little Doc. I watched him coming toward me. He was growing more like Father every day. He walked with Father's stride, his arms hung loose and awkward. His cowlick stuck up in front like Bill's, however. A shiver went down my spine.

Little Doc reached me. "Waiting for someone?"

"You."

He took my books and strapped them in with his. Then we walked down toward Main Street and the ten blocks home.

We passed the railroad station, Clendenin School, the grocery store. We talked about everything except what I was waiting for. We reached the woods just beyond our house before I asked it.

"Little Doc, remember the time we swiped Mother's butcher knife and cut our fingers with it to sign a pledge in blood?"

He laughed. "Still got the scar."

We had been twelve and thirteen years old, the blood-and-thunder years of *Beau Geste,* Edgar Allan Poe, Sabatini. Our pledge had been written on an old music diploma, signed in blood, buried by the tap root of an old oak tree in the heart of the woods. It had been worded most dramatically: " . . . to carry on the torch handed down to me, the third Physician in line, Robert Anderson Clayborne, and to me, the third Musician in line, Mary Myrtle Clayborne . . ."

"Still going to be the doctor that you were then?" I asked Little Doc.

He hesitated before answering. Only a half moment—then he grinned. "What do you think?" was all that he said, but it told me all that I had wanted to know.

When we reached home, I went directly to the dining-room table, for the letter that I knew would be waiting for me. The table was bare.

"No mail?" I asked casually.

"On your dresser," Mother answered, just as casually. How could she have known?

I put my books on the windowseat and went slowly upstairs. I closed my bedroom door behind me and leaned against it. There was the letter, propped up against the lamp on my dresser. It was from Bill, asking me to marry him. I wasn't worried any more about what to say to him. Little Doc had given me the answer.

Mother went to bed right after supper that night. Her face had been pale again. She still had a hacking cough in her chest.

Little Doc went back to his owl after his studying. Melie Kate and Ruth did their lessons before the fire, heard their Br'er Rabbit story, and went upstairs by themselves. When they left, I sat on the footstool by Father's feet.

"Father, I'd like to tell you something."

"All right. What is it?"

"Well—" My heart pounded. "I got a letter from Bill today. Now that he's almost through school, he wants me to marry him next spring." I looked down at my hands and finished quickly. "What I wanted to tell you is that I do love him after all, and I want to marry him."

"Well, now." Father settled lower in his chair and stretched his legs far in front of him. "I suppose you've told Mother?"

I shook my head. "No. I thought I should tell you first, after what I said on the swing that night. I thought maybe you would think I was being—silly."

"What changed your mind?" There was something joking in his manner—yet, he was serious. He wasn't teasing me.

"Oh, I think maybe the way Bill first asked me to marry him." I clasped my hands around my knees. "This was easier than I thought. "We rode down to Job's Landing, and we sat on the pier where we used to fish—and we were just talking."

"You think you'd rather marry Bill than study to be a piano teacher?"

"Oh—that." I breathed deeply. "I don't know whether I really want that or not, Father. The more I think about it, the more it's—" I should have practiced my words more. "—well, I really want to get married, that's what I really want." Father didn't answer, and I laughed in the awkward silence. "It was so funny, at the pier, Father. Bill didn't even kiss me. He slapped me. Three mosquitoes were chewing my face up and I didn't even feel it."

"Mosquitoes, eh?"

"Huge things—big enough to roast, Bill said."

Father chuckled. "Must have been baby dinosaurs to be able to navigate in all the oil in Black Hollow nowadays."

"Oh, no. Black Hollow was full of water."

He chuckled again and looked toward the fire. "Yep I guess you must really be in love. Black Hollow's been dry as a bone for two years."

"No, Father. It's full of water. The drainage from the lakes on Newcastle Hill backs in down there."

He turned and looked at me sharply. "What about the lakes on Newcastle Hill?"

"Everybody knows it. A lot of the boys at school go down there to catch frogs."

"Isn't it even oiled?"

I shook my head. "No. Is it supposed to be?"

"Of course it's supposed to be. Even dry, the place was to be kept oiled. It's a vicious mosquito-breeding place in that swamp." Suddenly he sat straight up in his chair and whistled through his teeth. "Scott! Why didn't I think of it before! Anopheles as thick as hops and nobody knowing where they were coming from—" He shoved his chair back and stood up. "Come along if you don't have anything else to do. I'm taking a ride down to Job's Landing. We can discuss your problem when we get back."

Father parked the car where the old wagon road ended by Three-Pipes' house, and we walked down to the pier. The swamp didn't look the same at night. Three-Pipes' house stood ashen gray and sullen. The slime around the banks shone green-gold in the moonlight. Frogs hushed their thrumming at our approach. Cicadas were stilled. Even the willow trees watched us stealthily.

Father turned his flashlight on the water. A turtle on a jagged stump eyed us with gold eyes, then slid into the thick water. All around, everywhere the light flashed, the water quivered with larvae and water bugs. Mosquitoes hit us in the face as we turned and walked back to the car again.

Father had said nothing. Now he was silent all the way home. His eyes were hard on the road ahead; his profile was lost in thought.

At home he strode directly into the library and switched the light on.

"Father," I said hesitantly, at the door.

He turned. "Yes?"

"You didn't give me your blessing, Father. I want to write Bill tonight."

"Come here, Mary."

I walked over to him. He turned me to look through the door, over toward the staircase. His bony finger pointed. "Last night a pitcher with big ears sat on that fourth step. Tonight that pitcher is trying to be a noble Grecian urn. You write Bill that you're only seventeen years old. Tell him that your ogre-parents won't even give their consent to your having a mind of your own on the question of marriage until you're eighteen." His voice lost its banter and was serious. "Promise me, Sister."

"Yes, Sir."

"A lot can happen in a year. Now go write your letter. Study your trigonometry while you're at it. I've found some work of my own to do."

# VIII

ON MONDAY MORNING, I was the last one downstairs for breakfast. Father had already left for the office.

The dining-room was charged with excitement.

"Hey, Sister, look! Look what Father did!"

It blazed on the front page. "COALS TO NEWCASTLE. North Side Doctor Flays City Health Authorities."

Melie Kate and Ruth were so excited that their pigtails stuck straight out. "Read it, Little Doc. Read it out loud!"

Little Doc cleared his throat. He stuck out his chest and leaned back in his chair. "To the Editor. Dear Sir: It has just come to my attention that spring is in full bloom again. Long underwear has been shed. Mosquitoes, like legislators, begin to introduce their little bills. . . ."

Ruthie bent over her plate and pealed with laughter.

Little Doc looked at her.

"She doesn't have the slightest idea what a legislator is," I remarked, around the edge of the paper.

"Yes, I have," Ruthie answered. "Like Papa wrote. They've got bills that they stick you with."

"She knows more than either of you," Mother said. "Read on, Little Doc."

When we all met at the table again, at supper time, Father took one look at us, tipped his chair back on two legs, and roared with laughter. There we sat, the four of us, a beautiful black eye apiece.

"Well, Father—" Four explanations began at once.

He let his chair down and banged on his water glass with a fork. "All right now."

We were still.

"What happened, Ruth?"

"Well!" She took a deep breath. "I had the newspaper first and I was cutting it out for my scrapbook, and then Melie Kate came and said that she had asked for it first and if I didn't give it to her she'd cut it in little bitty pieces, and—" She took another breath. "So I hit her!"

"And so Melie hit her back," Little Doc said.

Melie Kate was indignant. "I asked Mother for it."

"Who got it?" Father asked.

"Mother did!

"I was the biggest," Mother said serenely. Her face was trying hard not to be self-conscious tonight. The quirk was on her mouth again.

"I knocked a guy cold over it," Little Doc said. "Man! I wish you could have seen that." He snapped his fingers. "Laid him out just like that. Wasn't even late to my paper route."

"That kick to your eye must have been reflex action," Father said.

Little Doc shrugged deprecatingly. "Oh, he wasn't so bad—he's a good guy, anyway. It was his dad. Don said that he swore at you from one end of the house to the other this morning. He said that you didn't have any idea what you were spouting off about—that there never was anything in the appropriation bill about *keeping* Black Hollow drained." His eyes narrowed. "And he said that you and Editor Ben Taylor were thick as fleas. That you got it plastered on the front page for free publicity."

Father unfolded his napkin. "Too bad I have to shear myself of all this glory," he said dryly. "That front-page 'publicity' was Ben Taylor's idea of a joke. He's waited to use that headline ever since Newcastle Hill was opened up. My letter to The People's Column happened to be the first chance that walked under it."

"Look!" I said. "It seems that someone might ask me how I got my black eye."

"All right. What happened?"

"I was looking through a window." I leaned forward eagerly. "Look, Father—when we were at Job's Landing last Friday night, there wasn't any oil on the water, was there?"

"No."

"You're sure there wasn't?

He waited to answer. "Yes, I'm sure."

"Well, there is now!" I sat up straight. "It's oiled as slick as a whistle. Nan Mary and I rode out in her car after school, just for curiosity, and there's oil as far down as we could see. More than that, there are three big oil drums inside Three-Pipes' shack. That's how the eye—Nan Mary was holding me up so I could look in through the boards across the window—"

"The oil drums could have been there all the time," Father interrupted. "We didn't look."

"We thought about that, too." I said. "Then Nan Mary discovered that the door had been forced open either yesterday or today, because the lock wasn't dusty. And there were tracks on the porch."

"Something sounds funny to me," Little Doc said. "It was a funny thing, too, why Don's Dad got so sore about it. He's the State Highway Commissioner—he's not connected with the Board of Health."

"Children," Mother said quietly. "Do you realize that we haven't said grace yet?"

Next morning, at breakfast, Little Doc had another letter to read from the front page of the *Gazette*. It was Hudson Kaley's answer to Father's letter.

"It is time that someone took an interest in the health of the people outside the city limits," it began—smooth as the oil on Black Hollow.

Little Doc looked up from the paper. "Now what do you know about that?"

Father's eyes were dancing. "Did some investigating yesterday and found out that he's one of the promoters of Newcastle Hill. He owns tons of real-estate up there. So—he probably decided it might be better to come over to our side." He held up a warning finger at Little Doc's excited face. "This news doesn't go outside the front door!"

"Yes, sir."

Little Doc was waiting at the steps for me after school was out that afternoon.

"All examinations finished!" I greeted him gaily. "Come Friday night and I'm a graduated woman."

"We're to go down to Father's office before we go home," he said, taking my books.

"Why?"

"I don't know why. They sent me a note from the Principal's office this morning. He had called for us to come down as soon as school was out."

"I suppose it's something about Black Hollow."

"I don't know what it's about, Sister."

There were three patients waiting, when we reached the office, and we had to wait half an hour to see Father.

As we sat there, another thought came to me. Suppose he had called us in to say that he was going to take the chair at Missouri State University, after all! But as I looked around the room, I knew that Mother was right. The shabby, old-fashioned office; the high bookcases by the door; the dusty, stuffed animals; the Indian arrow collection mounted on beaverboard and hung on the side walls; the squeak of the swivel in the inner office; the faces waiting on the worn bench—this was Father here.

He would never fit behind a shining desk, with neat geometrical rows of faces spread before him.

The door to the inner office opened, and the last face from the bench was gone. A few minutes more, and Father opened the door again and motioned us in.

He pulled two chairs up to his desk. "Examinations go all right?" he asked me.

"I think so. I'll know better when I go up to get my diploma Friday night."

He sat in his swivel chair and squeaked it back as far as it would go. He swung it around until he faced us. "I'm afraid I've some pretty bad news for you this time."

"Black Hollow!" Little Doc said.

"No, no." He drummed his fingers on the arm of the chair. "It's your mother. She's not well." I remembered her face that was still so thin and white, the cough that didn't leave. "She's not seriously ill, remember that—there's nothing to get worried about—but I've decided that the wisest thing to do right now is to take her up to Booneville for a couple of months' rest."

It was a long stunned moment before we realized exactly what he meant. Little Doc said, "That's the tuberculosis sanitarium."

Father nodded. He swung his chair around to face the desk, and tapped his finger on a typewritten sheet before him. "It's only a spot on one lung—very, very small, but the sooner she gets up there the better. I called Dr. Shipton at the sanitarium last week. One vacancy comes up this Friday, so I took it for Myrtle. She doesn't know it yet." He turned and grinned dryly at Little Doc. "Reckon you'd better dust off your Boy Scout Manual when you get home. Looks as if we'll have some fancy hog-tying to do Friday morning."

So, Friday morning, as quickly as that, Father and Mother left for the tuberculosis sanitarium at Booneville. She was to be gone for all of the summer, perhaps even longer.

She was still angry about it. "Not one of them know what they're talking about," she declared impatiently. "I'll be back in a month. Nothing a doctor likes better than to turn flu into something complicated. Melie Kate and Ruth, you'll have to sit up proud when Sister graduates tonight. You're taking Mama and Papa's places, you know. Little Doc, don't let Ruthie take her shoes off."

Melie Kate and Ruth had presents for her. Ruthie had trudged to the store the afternoon before, a dime that Little Doc had given her tied in the corner of her handkerchief. She had come back with a loaf of bread. "She'll get hungry, Sister. Put some jelly on it."

Melie Kate spent her dime on a ring with a diamond the size of a marble. It glittered brilliantly on Mother's little finger as she waved until the car turned at Main Street.

When the car disappeared beyond the line of houses, we turned and went in the house again. Ruth went on to play, but Melie Kate stayed indoors to read.

Later in the morning, I found Melie in tears under the piano, far over in the corner.

"Oh, Honey, come on out. Mother's coming back. Come on out—we'll find Ruthie and make some roads in the woods."

She sobbed and sobbed against my shoulder. "I had a bigger one for her, Sister. I had a great big diamond picked out and the woman in the store wrapped up the wrong one."

# IX

JULY 6TH WAS Ruthie's seventh birthday.

Mother sent her a card, addressed to her "firecracker who exploded two days late," and I put it under her plate at the supper table.

"Wait until she sees this," I said to Little Doc.

He was looking toward the living-room. "Wait until you see *this*," he said, dryly.

Melie Kate came through the door, Ruth behind her.

"Ruth!" I shrieked. "Oh, Ruthie, what happened to your hair?"

"I got it cut," she said.

"It's what she really wanted for her birthday," Melie Kate said, "so I gave it to her."

They calmly pulled their stools up to the table. It was a moment before I could speak. "Oh, you did! Just since when did you take over the authority here?"

"I'm nine years old. I'm over nine years old. And Sister, I've told you over and over and over—Ruthie doesn't look right with braids. Now she looks pretty."

"Something ought to be done about the hemline," Little Doc put in.

"The scissors weren't much good," Ruth said apologetically.

I was disgusted. "Just look at her! You'd think she's had scurvy. Well! I haven't time to even it off now. Go tell Father that supper's ready."

I went back to the kitchen, and Ruthie went to the library to get Father. Mother had picked the wrong firecracker; Melie Kate was the one who smoldered silently behind a serene and lovely face.

There was a letter from Mother, and I read it aloud after Father said grace. She said she loved the fresh air, the mattresses, and the sheets that smelled of pine and sunshine. She loved the mountain in front of the porch where she lay in the sun all day. She loved Dr. Shipton and she loved Dr. Barton. In fact, she was having a wonderful and lazy vacation, and if all Ruth's teeth were still growing in straight, and I was watching that Melie Kate played outdoors a lot instead of staying indoors to draw and paint all day, she wouldn't even bother to worry—she would be home before school started, anyway.

Father frowned when I laid the letter down.

"It will be a long time after school starts before she gets home," he said. "Shipton said six months at best. My guess is that it will be much longer."

Longer than six months! Summer, autumn, winter—

"Does that mean that she's worse than you thought?" Little Doc asked.

Father shook his head. "No. It means that it takes a long time to get rid of a T.B. spot. She'll be good to be home by spring."

Spring! All through the winter. All winter long! All winter long! The cruel, selfish thought beat on me like a hammer stroke.

Father spoke. "I thought that maybe in the fall you could start lessons from Professor Howell, Sister—" He hesitated.

I kept my eyes on my plate. "Thank you, Father."

"All winter long!" the hammer stroke repeated. I ate over a burning lump in my throat. Only now, for the first time, did I fully realize that there was to be no Conservatory this winter. I had still carried faith for a miracle. Now, even if the money had been there, I couldn't leave. I had to stay home all winter long.

"Sister, Sister—" Ruthie pulled my sleeve.

"What do you want?"

She was indignant. "I've asked you three times, Sister. I want the ham and eggs, please."

I passed the platter to her, and looked back at my plate again. I didn't want anyone to see my eyes. Suddenly I was hating that word "Sister" that chained me to long, bitter months.

The meal went on, and I talked to somebody. Then, all at once, I laid my fork on my plate. Where was my faith, that I thought a winter had to be bitter and empty, merely because a plan of mine had reached a stone wall? There were paths around stone walls. Professor Howell was a new teacher here, from England and Trinity College—Mother had said that he was excellent. A year studying here, and I would still be only eighteen when the next autumn came. Mother had been twenty before she left for her Conservatory.

"You know," I said, looking at Father, "I think I'd like to study from Professor Howell. Mother thinks he'd be wonderful for theory and counterpoint. I can get all the history from the library, myself. With Melie Kate and Ruth in school all day, that means hours of practice here with no one to interrupt. Yes," I said. "I would like that. Thank you!"

Father's eyes were sharp on me. I looked straight back at him. Then he grinned and his big hand went up to his forehead. "Salute, Skipper," it was saying to me. I grinned in return and picked up my fork again.

When supper was finished, Father laid his napkin on the table and pushed his chair back. "Well!" He stood up. "Better get back to work." He gave his trousers a hitch and clumped through the living-room, back to the library. The door closed behind him.

"What is he doing in that room that's so important?" Little Doc asked me.

I put the lid back on the butter dish. "I don't know. He hasn't allowed me in there to dust, for days. There's papers all over the place. All his law books are down—all his medical files—stacks of back issues of the *Gazette*. Once I moved a tiny piece of paper from the top of the bookcase, and he tore around breathing fire at me all evening. Everything in there is untouchable."

"He's untouchable, too," Little Doc said.

Melie Kate and Ruth pushed their stools under the table. "Can we play until dark, Sister?"

"Not until we do a job on Ruth's hair," I said. "Go get the scissors out of Mother's sewing-box, Ruth."

The summer plodded on, hot and sultry and slow. Dust from the road made a choking, yellow cloud whenever a car drove past.

Melie Kate grew taller, Ruthie grew plumper. Little Doc was burned as brown as mahogany from his hours in the sun, and he already stood a good head over me. In July he started work in Frank's Sandwich Shop, across the street from the high school. When school started, he was to work from four in the afternoon until eight o'clock at night.

The library grew dustier and more cluttered. Father worked in there almost every evening. We had done very little reading together this summer.

Then one evening the doorbell rang, and two men stood there that I had never seen before. Mr. Saunders and Mr. Pitzel. Father came from the library to greet them. The three of them went into the library together, and it was long after eleven o'clock before I heard Father walk to the porch and say goodnight.

The next evening, the eminent lawyer, Tom Harding Hammond, stood at the door when Saunders and Pitzel rang the doorbell. He stalked in with his briefcase. Around midnight he stalked out again.

For the rest of that month, the doorbell rang almost every evening after supper. The men, Saunders and Pitzel, wiped the perspiration from their brows with big monogrammed handkerchiefs and laughed wearily. "When your father gets his head set on something, he's a veritable devil, Miss Clayborne, a veritable devil!" Tom Harding Hammond stalked in and out, a tall, solemn stick of a man.

If a call from back country came while the four men were closeted in the library, Father would stride out, his sparse iron-gray hair standing on end where his hands had been going through it, his baggy pants barely staying their half-way up, his rubbers clumping him upstairs to change his clothes to go on the call.

"Doesn't that man ever say 'goodnight'?" one of the men finally asked the other one night.

"Never heard him. Never says 'goodbye,' either. He phones and says, 'Saunders, coming over tonight?' I say, 'Well, now, yes, I reckon if you think—' He says 'same time,' and bang! the receiver's up. I sit there feeling like a durned fool."

They shook their heads and turned at the door to bid me goodnight. Only Tom Harding Hammond had no comment to make upon Father's brusqueness.

# X

BILL CAME BACK the first week in September.

I was washing the dining-room windows that morning. I stood on Melie Kate's footstool, outside the windowseat, and had just reached in through the open window for the chamois on the windowseat when I heard the quick step on the front path, then the leap to the porch.

"Bill!" I called, excitedly.

I could see through to the front door. "Hey, come on back, Bill. It's housecleaning day."

He sauntered through into the dining-room, his hands in his pockets, the cowlick combed down slickly. He grinned. "Hi, Spareribs."

"Hello." For an embarrassed second I wondered how I should feel around him now—he had never commented upon my answer to his letter. Then, "Bill!" I shrieked. "You've got a mustache. Oh, how funny!"

He sat on the windowseat. "You might give it a chance, Lady. It's only a month old."

"I don't like it anyway."

"Neither do I like the way you keep growing. Is that your height in stocking feet?" He leaned his head out the window to look at my feet. "Oh," he said, relievedly, when he saw the stool. "Some way, I'd never fancied a wife seven feet tall."

My face prickled. For a second his voice had not been joking in the words—his head was too close to mine.

I drew back on my stool. "Look, Bill. It's almost time to get dinner, and I want to get these windows finished since they're already soaped. Suppose you go in the living-room and read a book for about five minutes."

I started to close the window, but Bill reached over and pushed it up again. "No, no. My news won't wait. Here, I'll give you a hand up—the windows can wait."

He reached for my hand and pulled me through the open window and onto the windowseat.

"Oh, dear," I said. "That tore my dress. I heard it split."

"That was me, bursting with news," Bill said. "Sit up straight and listen."

I leaned against the side wall, and Bill grinned. "Come to think about it, it might not all be news after all. I imagine that Big Doc has told you part of it."

"Part of what?"

"Well, first of all, that I'm not coming back here to practice with him."

My heart missed a beat. "Oh, Bill, no—" Father had dreamed for Bill's shingle under his, as much as he had ever dreamed for Little Doc's. "Bill—you can't—"

He looked away and rumpled his hair. "I'm staying in St. Louis and going into plastic surgery with Dr. Ledbetter." He laughed self-consciously. "You might quit looking so palsied, Spareribs. It cramps my style."

I looked down at the chamois in my hand. "Father didn't tell me a word about it. I guess if I'd stopped to think about it though, I'd have known Easter that you weren't coming back."

"It was the very devil to tell him, Mary, you know it was. You're making it ten times worse."

"I'm sorry."

His hands went through his hair again, and I knew the cowlick would be standing straight up. "You know, Mary, if you'd stop to think about a few other things, you'd see that I don't fit in down there in that office at all. I don't even fit this town. Your father would look just about as funny in a cocktail bar."

"I don't know. Father might be fun in a cocktail bar."

"You've never seen a cocktail bar."

"I've read about them."

"Oh, come out of your books, Lady." He was impatient. "Doctors aren't the same, any more than people are the same. Big Doc belongs here because he understands the type of patient who is here—I belong in Ledbetter's office because I understand the type of patient who is there. If I had to go dashing around cutting off toes for a cord of wood, and delivering babies for a bunch of carrots, I'd despise it in a month. I'm not cut of that cloth, that's all—I'm in a different groove."

I said, "What kind of groove?"

"Ledbetter's kind of groove. Specializing, for one thing. I want steady hours and steady pay, too." He tapped his foot on the floor. "I love medicine, but there's so many other things that I want to get out of life, too. I want time for that."

I looked up at him. He looked back at me, his eyes eager and intense. And there had been nothing cocky in his voice—nothing false.

"Ledbetter's the biggest man in plastic surgery in this section of the country," he said. "He wants to retire in two years, and then his whole practice would be in my hands. Ledbetter knows that I can do it. I know I can, too. Just look, Spareribs, everything I've ever worked for, right here in my two hands."

I asked, "What have you worked for, Bill?"

"What every man works for—the right job to do, the right place to live, the right people to know." He hesitated. "The right sort of wife to go along with him, too. We could have everything we want, you and I. I think I'm going to be quite a rich guy." I only looked at him. He said, "I'm really very serious about it. We'd have plenty for you to go to your music school—" He laughed. "When you hit eighteen and get around to deciding what you're going to do with me, you can remember that I'm throwing in the Conservatory with it."

I looked down at the chamois again. "Thank you, Bill. That's not my way of getting it." Something was beginning to tremble in me.

Bill leaned forward. "Look, Spareribs, I want to give you everything that you want so badly. I know what you want. You want big things to hear, big people to meet, big things to do, too— I can get them for you. You don't belong here. No more than I do."

I didn't look up. "How do you know what I want, Bill?"

"I've known ever since you were six years old. It follows you around like a shadow. We have the same sort of dream—you'll make the same choice that I did when it comes your time."

The trembling in me was becoming anger. "You've always been wrong about me, Bill. I don't want to be a concert pianist—I'm not that sort of person. I just want to be a—a teacher—" Suddenly it sounded humble, trite.

He laughed. "All right then. You can be a teacher. But you can be the biggest teacher in St. Louis. You can sit under the biggest degree on the wall. You can have the biggest Steinway in the biggest studio—"

"That isn't what I want, Bill."

"Of course it's what you want. How do you know what you want? You've never been outside Arkansas in your life. You can name the price you want some day—choose the pupil you want—"

I couldn't keep the trembling out of my voice much longer. "I didn't know there was such a thing as a 'right pupil' to have."

"Of course there's a right pupil. You don't have to teach just anyone if you're good enough—"

My anger exploded. I shook all over. "Mother never chose a pupil in her life. Grandfather never chose a pupil. My father never chose a patient. I don't know what you're talking about. Mother teaches a little half-wit boy named Rickie, that no other teacher in town would look at, and it's the most beautiful lesson that I've ever seen—"

"Hey, here, wait a minute—" Bill was laughing at me.

"I won't wait a minute for anybody. Go on back to St. Louis—you don't know what you're talking about. Go on away!"

"My first proposition to a lady, and my ears are slapped back!"

"Go on away, Bill!" I wanted to scream at him. "Go on!"

He left the windowseat without another word, and I sat there looking out the window, my body taut from something that had struck electricity from every spark of me. I was ashamed—but it wasn't the first time that Bill had done that to me. From the time that I had been a little girl, I would find myself suddenly trembling with fury before the mocking laughing wall of his words in front of me. Once, in that anger, I had struck him with my tennis racket. The scar was still on his forehead.

Swiftly I left the windowseat and ran into the living-room. "Bill! Bill!"

He sat on the front steps. He didn't turn around when I came up. "Bill, I'm sorry." My throat hurt with remorse now. "You meant to be kind, Bill. I don't know why I get angry at you—I always do and I don't want to."

"Don't let it worry you. I'm used to it."

All remorse left me. His voice wasn't even ruffled. He had only come out on the steps to wait for me. Bill knew me too well!

I sat on the steps beside him. "Thank you for trying to give me something that you thought I wanted, anyway. I'll always remember it."

"You'll take it later. You haven't grown up yet."

"All right, now, Bill. My temper's being controlled."

He reached down and picked up a twig from the step. I took a deep breath. "Goodness, but we'll miss you around here, Bill. I don't know what Father will do without you there to laugh with him."

"It's not easy for me to do without him, either. This wasn't an easy thing to decide. He's practically been my father, too."

"Well, don't worry about it. He knows that you wouldn't be staying there if you didn't know that it was right for you. Mother will know it, too."

He broke the twig in little pieces and dropped them on the step below. "A man can always find the right answer when the right people say that."

"Well," I said, standing up, "I can't stay here any longer. I have to start dinner. Look—if you'll get out the dried apples, we'll have schnitz and knepf for dessert."

# XI

SCHOOL STARTED. Melie Kate and Ruth went the seven blocks to and from Clendenin every day; Little Doc went the half-mile farther to the high school. Professor Howell's classes in theory and counterpoint began—but I wasn't in them. Something had happened to change my mind about accepting a compromise for my dream. I would wait until I could go to the Conservatory. Even if it meant a year, I could wait—I had found a feeling to carry me until then.

The feeling had begun when I overheard a conversation in the Church Circle room one afternoon, soon after Bill had gone back to St. Louis.

I had baked cookies for the meeting, as Mother used to do, and I stayed to help Emma Wilson serve. The swinging door into the other room, where the women were sewing for the new poor family, brought their voices clearly into the kitchen where I was. Emma went to the pantry for trays, and Mrs. Hammond's voice suddenly stood out in my consciousness.

"I think everybody's watching to see what will happen, Mrs. Royal. I'd never have said she could do it. She's not the type, that's all. John has always said to me, he says lots of times on the way home from church, 'Jen, she gives me the creeps sometimes. I look down from the choir and see her sitting there at the piano and she no more belongs sitting down there than anything. She just don't belong'—"

"She don't belong in this town, that's what it is."

Mrs. Hammond's voice softened. "Well, I guess she belongs here now, poor thing. Bringing up two little sisters, and doing the cooking and the housework. Every time I bake, I say, 'John, I'm going to take half this cake over to the Claybornes—that poor lamb can't do everything—' "

Emma suddenly took the plate of cakes from my hands and laughed loudly. "You watch that coffee over there, Mary, or it won't be fit to pour down the sink. I'll go on and take the cakes in, no?"

She was gone through the door. It swung back and forth behind her. The voices were stilled in the other room.

That was the first thread of the new feeling. All the way home from the church, afterwards, it unraveled farther and farther from my mind. Someone else had said that I didn't belong in this town. What had Bill said?

"You want big places to go, big things to do, too—" At this moment I should be hundreds of miles away, taking my lesson in the narrow bare room with the black Steinway, walking down the corridors lined with muted sounds from the practice rooms, sitting in my own room for the hours of study that I was so hungry for, hearing the concerts that drowned me in their sounds—those glorious concerts that Mother told me about. They had never come to Arkansas.

Instead of that, I was walking up Maple Street, leaving the church early so that I could be home when Melie Kate and Ruth got in from school. In another hour there would be supper to start—after supper, school lessons to help with, stories from school to listen to, dishes to wash, two little sisters to put to bed and get ready for school the next day. Who at home realized what it meant to me to do that? No one ever said a word.

Until that moment, this year had been a year of waiting for me. Hadn't Father spoken of Jacob's seven years for Rachel? Now, all in a moment, it became a year bathed in a new feeling. People in the houses were looking out and saying, "You'd never know it to look at her, would you? Think of the bitter disappointment in her heart, yet she goes on as if she loves it. She'll be paid for it some day."

"Sister—Sister!" Someone was calling me.

A block back on Maple Street, running to catch up with me, were Melie Kate and Ruth coming home from school. "Wait, Sister!"

I stood still until they reached me. Melie Kate's eyes shone and her voice was happy with excitement. "Sister, wait until you hear. I'm in a play at school. Our first play. Wait until I show you!" She laid her schoolbooks on the sidewalk and flipped through the pages of one of the books. "Sister, I made up my own goblin costume, and my art teacher says— Oh, Sister— just you wait—"

"Well, I can't wait now," I said, impatiently. "And you'll ruin your book on the dirty sidewalk like that. Bring it on home and show me later."

"I'll find it in a minute—"

"Not here, Melie Kate. Pick up your books and come on."

I started on down the street, and in a moment Melie Kate and Ruth followed me. They were very quiet all the way home, and so was I. My mind had gone back to the conversation in the church room.

Then it was late October. Indian summer, and the world was mellow in the heavy sunshine, the sharp blue sky, the lazy smell of leaf smoke drifting across the yard. The hickory tree by Little Doc's window was a great golden torch.

One Saturday, we took Melie Kate and Ruth to Aunt Melie's to spend the day, and Father, Little Doc and I started down the Tom Box road back country, to go to Letty Granther's wedding.

I sat in the back seat of the car to keep my eye on the cherry pie, still steaming from the oven.

"What's that for?" Little Doc asked.

"For the wedding supper."

"Did Omie tell you to bring it?"

"She told Father to tell me that all the unmarried girls were bringing a cherry pie for the supper. Something about 'Can she bake a cherry pie, Billy Boy, Billy Boy?' Perhaps my future husband will be there and he'll recognize me then by the taste of my cherry pie."

Little Doc's laugh was scoffing. "I can just bet. Imagine someone walking up to Sister and saying, 'Hello, future wife!' She'd sail past with all sails hoisted."

"All right now, Little Doc," I said. "Cut it out."

He turned clear around in the front seat and faced me. "No joking, Sister, what's happened that you're so snooty lately? Dean Ryan told me he's asked you three times to go somewhere with him lately and you've been busy every time."

I merely looked back at him.

"Dean's a good guy," Little Doc persisted. "Isn't anybody good enough for you to go with around here any more? What's the matter with Dean?"

I was sarcastic. "Nothing's the matter with Dean—he's buck-toothed and he talks like a ninny. Nobody in this town has any more ambition than to make ten dollars a week and get married right off the bat. You leave me alone and take care of your own love affairs."

"Tut, tut, Sister," Father said. "Curb your tongue."

"Well, why doesn't he leave me alone about getting married? That's all he and Mother can talk about."

"Be still, now."

I stared sullenly out the window. Little Doc turned back in his seat, still laughing. It seemed that nobody cared how I felt any more—not even Father.

I didn't say another word until the car reached Phineas Granther's house, and Father parked the car alongside the trucks and old Fords and

wagons in the oak grove. Little Doc jumped out of the car and opened the
back door for me. He grinned at me. I got out without looking at him
again, and walked toward the house by myself.

Old Phineas came out on the porch, his face beaming, his beady eyes
twinkling. The rancor in my heart melted when he held out his wrinkled
yellow hand to me.

"We're honored that ye come today, Miss Mary."

"I'm honored that you asked me, Mr. Granther."

Father and Little Doc had reached the porch, and Old Phineas turned
from me. He laid a hand on Little Doc's shoulder. "The boy's gettin' to be
a tall 'un, Big Doc," he said proudly to Father. "We ain't got long to wait
fer 'im now."

"Another year and he starts medical school," Father said. "He'll come
back and cure your arthritis yet, Phineas."

Old Phineas chuckled. "He'll be better'n his Pa if he does."

He hobbled down the steps, and he and Father and Little Doc started
down the path that led to the orchard. The altar and wedding benches were
set up down there today.

A little girl came running up on the porch behind me. "Hey, Aint
Becky!" she called into the house. "Aint Becky! Lookit! Preacher's
comin'! He's comin' on a horse!"

Women's faces crowded to the windows. They looked right past me,
back to the road. Voices buzzed. "Hit's young Preacher MacCreighton.
Come to Granite Hill last spring when Preacher Evans died." "Tall 'un,
ain't he? 'Nother boot length and he'd be scrapin' dirt."

I turned to look back to the road, too. The horseman had reached the
top of the third of the five hills. The sun struck gold from the saddle, the
horses' hoofs made sharp puffs of yellow dust from the road. I turned and
went into the house, into the front room. The women stayed by the
window. No one turned to pay any attention to me. "His Ma come from
Scotland, Effie Johnson said," one voice said. Another tongue clucked
sadly. "Him most thirty years old and not married yet. A shame, hit is."
"He lives in the old Barrington house all by hisself."

They talked on, so I went to the kitchen. Omie was standing by the
stove. She wiped the perspiration from her swarthy face and laughed her
hearty laugh. "Well, look who's brung a cherry pie to ketch herse'f a man.
Ain't they enough men in the town to suit ye, girl?"

"Oh, there's enough. They aren't good-looking enough, Omie."

Her laugh was shriller. "Listen at 'er. Piece of her Pa's tongue she's got." She motioned toward the table. "Set it on down and git on down to the orchard afore the weddin' starts. Won't be but a minute now. Preacher's come."

I walked down the path that led from the back door to the orchard. The benches were almost half-full of people. Men stood and smoked under the trees, children romped and laughed in the clearing beyond the apple trees.

Father and Phineas sat on one of the benches, close to the front of the altar. Little Doc wasn't with them. I settled myself on the bench next to Father, as voices exploded in breathless whispers behind me.

"I seen her dress, Mildred," one of them said. "Hit's white and hit's got gourds in the skirt."

"What's gourds in a shirt?"

"Somethin' sort of flared-like. Letty copied it off'n one in a store winder in town. She said the girl in the store said hit was a weddin' dress with a gourd skirt."

A third voice spoke piously. "Jeff Glazer ain't takin' Letty's weddin' so good."

"He'll git all right."

"She shouldn't never a set in church with him all thet time if'n she didn't aim to stand up with him."

The first voice was lofty. "She did aim to marry Jeff 'till Eskar asked her. I know. She's my own first cousin."

"I know more'n thet and she ain't no kin of mine. I was thar when Eskar spoke to 'er."

The other two voices closed in. "What'd you hear, Mildred? We won't tell. Spit on a crosseyed cat!"

"Hit was at the singin' to Mount Zion after cotton pickin'." The voice lowered to a breathless undertone. "I was a-washin' my hands in the creek down behind the juniper bushes by the well, and here come Eskar and Letty fer a drink. When he was a-pullin' the bucket up, I heerd him say, 'Reckon ye'll have to stand pretty high on tiptoe when ye kiss me, Letty Granther,' and she said, 'I ain't never stood on tiptoe yet to kiss a man, Eskar Toler.' So he said, 'Well, I ain't a man too proud to stoop down,'— and then the well rope quit creakin'—" All three voices merged in exclamations.

"Sh!" One hissed. "Aint Becky's a-comin'."

"Time to start, I reckon."

Aunt Becky sat heavily on the bench in front of me and fanned herself with a paper fan. As if by signal, the men knocked their pipes against the trees, the children quieted and came toward the benches.

Little Doc came back. There was no room left on the bench by us by that time, so he laid his coat on the end of the bench and leaned against a tree by the side.

A moment later the minister came down the center aisle and stood behind the green-covered altar. Without looking at the crowd before him, he opened the huge Bible at the bookmark and stood waiting. The women in the house had been right—he was easily the tallest man in the grove. His coat sleeves were too short for him; his bony wrists protruded awkwardly.

A buzzing ran through the grove. Heads turned back to look up the path toward the house. Letty was coming! The grove was hushed. The only sound was the softness of her steps on the grassy aisle, the mute sound of bated breath from the benches—yet Letty walked to all the music ever written, all the soft words ever spoken. Eskar took her hand when she reached the pulpit and they turned and faced the minister together.

He looked up from his book then, and looked down on them. "Dearly beloved—" His deep voice filled the orchard.

It may have been the spell of Indian summer—it may have been the deep rich voice of the new minister, but the marriage words flowed to me, along my veins, into my heart. How could everyone banter about marriage? It was not for anyone to stand before the altar. Only those who walk the same path, hear the same song, dream the same dream. I would find the right man when it was time. It would be years from now, after school was finished and my work was found—it would be hundreds of miles from here. There was no man here for me.

The words flowed on. "If any man can show just cause why these two be not united in holy matrimony, let him speak now or forever hold his peace." The minister's voice paused. The orchard was breathless in the moment of waiting.

In this instant came the sharp crack of a gun.

A prickling wave swept over me. The sound still thundered in my ears—the echo bounded back from the hills beyond.

In a second, men had risen from the benches and were running toward the clearing at the side.

"Watch out fer 'is gun, Ormond. He's drunk. Head 'im off by the barn." Far in the distance, a man dropped a gun and ran for the woods. Suddenly he turned and ran toward the group of buildings by the barn.

"Over this 'away, Jake! You got 'im!"

I looked back at the altar. Eskar and Letty still stood as before. The minister still had his hands on the Bible. There was a crack of a twig under footsteps by my side, and I saw Little Doc reach over and take his coat from the end of the bench. He grinned and winked, but I turned back coldly. He could never quit teasing! Not any time.

The minister smiled crookedly and said, "I guess nothing counts for my question except spoken words. If no one else has anything to say, we'll go on where we left off."

The tension was relieved when he spoke. The faces on the benches smiled and settled back for the rest of the ceremony. When the last of the marriage words were spoken, however, and Letty had stood on tiptoe and Eskar's dark head had bent down to hers, whispered words broke loose all over the orchard. An undercurrent of anger rippled beneath the surface. People crowded up to the two at the altar, but the words went on.

"Hit was Jeff Glazer. I knowed he'd do somethin'!"

"Hit was Jeff, did ye hear? Jeff Glazer!"

"Drunk as a coot!"

"Drunk, nothin'! He don't aim thet straight when he's drunk."

"Jeff aims better when he's drunk."

"Hit's a wonder warn't no one hit by the side thar. Crazy damned fool!"

Omie's voice sounded shrill and loud over the others. "Come on down to the tables, folks. Food's waitin'. Bug's'll beat ye to it if ye don't git movin'!"

Footsteps started back up the path toward the back of the house where the tables stood. Eskar and Letty walked ahead, their eyes shining and embarrassed with love—the interruption of five minutes before already belonging to the past. Small boys slipped furtively up to the altar to look at the bullethole in the side of the green cloth.

I looked around for Father, but he was already gone. Little Doc was gone from the apple tree, too. Strange that both of them should leave me. I stood up on the bench to look over the heads of the people. Then I saw the two of them far up the path to the house, Father striding ahead, Little Doc behind. They turned off the path toward the oak grove. They must be going after something in the car.

A voice by my side startled me. "Would ye take an old man for a partner to the tables, Miss Mary?"

I laughed and stepped down from the bench. "You almost scared me,

Mr. Granther."

"Your men will be back."

"It's a funny feeling to be deserted by both of them."

He leaned on his long black cane, and we walked up the grassy path toward the tables.

"Big Doc tells me your good mother will be back come spring," Old Phineas said in a moment.

"Spring is a long time away," I answered.

He nodded. "Ah, but a good wind is good for one."

"Oh, I don't really mind," I said. "It isn't very hard. Only about six more months, and that's not so bad." I laughed apologetically. "My hands are getting red from dishwashing, though—that's not so good for a pianist."

We had gone all of a dozen steps more before he answered. "Be keerful the wind don't blow the grain away with the chaff."

His words came with no meaning to my ears—but then he was always talking in riddles. We had reached the tables by that time and he spoke to Omie. "Got a job you can give Big Doc's gal, Omie?"

Omie picked up a long flat knife. "She kin help at the pie table. Birdie's helpin' me here and if somebody don't watch, them little snot brat's'll git in them pies."

"I'll watch them," I said.

She handed me the knife and I went over to the pie table to stay until Father and Little Doc returned.

As soon as Letty and Eskar had cut their cake, and finished their talking, they left in Jake Talbot's truck to go to Grandma Toler's house. Father said, "A lot of the younger girls and boys are going down to the barn for a square dance, Sister. Do you want to stay or go home?"

"I want to stay," I said. "What does Little Doc want to do?"

"He says it's up to you."

"Let's stay for a while then. I've never been to a square dance."

Father hesitated. "Little Doc looks pretty tired."

"Oh, he's still mad. Just let him alone and he'll be all right."

Jake Granther with the black beard pulled one of the barrels into the middle of the floor when we reached the barn, and sat on it to tune his fiddle. Josh Barrington sat beside him with his jug.

"Let's git Josh to sing the rattlesnake song," someone called out loudly. "Sing the rattlesnake song, Josh, while everybody gits in."

Josh and Jake pulled the barrel over to the door, and Joshua was singing before Father and I had found boxes at the wall to sit on. His face was as solemn as an owl, his scratchy voice was a rolling monotone.

> "Once on a hi-wi-will
>   There lived a ma-wa-wan
> The nicest young ma-wa-wan
>   Thet ever did li-wi-wive.
>
> Tum rattle-tum-a-ru-da-ray."

> "One day this ma-wa-wan
>   Thought he would go-wo-wo
> Out into the mea-wea-weado
>   For to mow-wo-wow.
>
> Tum rattle-tum-a-ru-da-ray."

Voices began to join in on the one-line chorus. The bigger boys were bringing in benches from the orchard to set along the wall. We had to stand up to make room for them. Jake and Josh paid not the slightest attention to the interruption.

> "He had not mow-wo-wowed
>   Mor'n half across the fie-wie-wield
> Till a rattle-tum-sna-wa-wake
>   Come and bit him on his he-wee-weel.
>
> Tum rattle-tum-a-ru-da-ray."

> "Oh, Father dea-wea-wear
>   Go tell my gal-wal-wal,
> I'm going to die-wie-wie
>   For I know I sha-wa-wal
>
> Tum rattle-tum-a-ru-da-ray."

Dozens of voices had joined in the last line by this time. Girls giggled and crowded onto the benches. Little Doc sat on the other side of Father without a look at me. Josh sang on:

> "This kind old ma-wa-wan,
>   Soon spread the new-wew-wews

> And out skipped Sa-wa-wal
>   Without her sho-woe-woes—"

Omie stepped up beside Josh and joined in with a voice that swamped his,

> "Tum rattle-tum-a-ru-da-ray."

"Sing it, Omie, sing it—" Someone shouted.
She leaned back and sang as solemnly as Josh did,

> "Oh, Johnny dea-wea-wear
>   Why did you go-wo-wo
> Out into the mea-wea-weado
>   For to mo-wo-wow?

The crowd roared with her, "Tum rattle-tum-a-ru-da-ray!"
Father leaned over and almost yelled in my ear. "She's the only one in Ellis County who can call hogs with that verse." I laughed up at him, but he had already turned again and was clapping his hands and stomping his feet with the others. They were all singing now,

> "Oh, Sally dea-wea-wear
>   Did you not know-wow-wow
> When the grass gets high-wigh-wigh
>   It's bound to be mow-wow-wowed?
>
> Tum rattle-tum-a-ru-da-ray!"

> "Come all ye gal-wal-wals
>   And shed a tea-wea-wear
> For this young ma-wa-wan
>   Who died right here-wear-wear.
>
> Tum rattle-tum-a-ru-da-ray!"

> "Come all ye me-we-wen
>   And a lesson ta-wa-wake
> And never get bi-wi-wit
>   By a rattle-tum-sna-wa-wake!
>
> Tum rattle-tum-a-ru-da-ray!"

The voices lingered on and on for the last note, until it broke with a final shout, and Father's voice yelled with the rest of them. When he caught me looking at him, surprised, he turned and yelled again. "Give us the square dance now, Jake! Swing it high!"

Voices took it up. "Make it the Chicken Pepper, Jake!"

"Come call it, Omie!"

"Cain't no one call like Omie."

She protested furiously, but the crowd pushed her back, and finally she stood by Jake's elbow and cleared her voice to begin.

"Have you ever tried it?" a man's voice said by me. I looked up. It was the minister.

"I don't know—" I said.

Father reached behind me and pushed me up. "Take her away, Mr. MacCreighton. I don't dare lose my dignity when she keeps an eye on me."

I blushed to my ears. "I'll try," I said, without looking at Mr. MacCreighton. "I don't have any idea how the steps go, though."

He crooked one of his long arms. "The men do the work. All the women do is to hang on." I hooked my arm through his, and we pushed through the crowd until we reached Birdie Brant and Jess Barrington. They were waiting to make a square with us.

The fiddle screeched, Omie's voice called shrill and loud, and in a moment the dancing had become a whirling, turning mass of feet. I hung on to any arm that reached for me. I was dizzy and breathless, but when the music finally stopped, and the minister's long arm reached for me to keep me from falling, I was full of the exhilaration of the music.

"Oh, it's wonderful!" I laughed up at Mr. MacCreighton. "I've never spent such a crazy five minutes in my life before!"

He turned and pulled me through the crowd after him. "Wait until they work up a lather—better sit down and get your breath. It hasn't begun yet."

I sat down breathlessly on the bench again, and Mr. MacCreighton left me to join the older men who had come in to stay by the door. Father stayed where he was. He was chuckling to himself.

When the dance began the second time, one of the boys about my age leaned forward from where he had been leaning against the wall. He reached out his hand and spoke quickly and awkwardly, "Would you dance with me?" Mr. MacCreighton was still talking to the men by the door, so I put my hand in the boy's and walked out on the floor with him.

The dancing really began with that dance. The fiddle had become a groove of screeching melody: the jug made deep bullfrog tones. The dancing went on and on, and I danced on and on, one partner after another for a square. The girls and women on the benches were watching me: all the eyes were watching me. I danced in a glow of exhilaration. No one else had had as many partners as I.

Father came over to me between one of the rounds. "Think we'd better go now, Sister. It's pretty late."

"One more, Father. This will be the last one."

He turned and went back to the bench. I glanced at Little Doc. He sat in the same place that he had been all afternoon. There was a smile on his face as he watched the people—but it wasn't his usual smile. He was still sulking! I turned back to the group of boys around me. "I think I'll dance with Johnny. He's been waiting since Joshua cracked his jug." I laughed and held out my hand to him.

He grinned self-consciously, and I said, "Tell me what happened to Jeff Glazer, Johnny."

"They put him to bed," Johnny answered in a low voice. "He jest got drunk."

"You mean they put him to bed in Mr. Granther's house?"

"More'n that, they put him in Letty's room."

I pealed with laughter. "Oh, that was mean!"

The jug boomed, the fiddle screeched, and the last dance had begun. I looked around, but Mr. MacCreighton had left. I knew that every other eye was watching me as Johnny and I swung off to the side in the first step.

It was dark by the time we had collected Melie Kate and Ruth at Aunt Melie's, and started home. The girls were so sleepy that they could hardly stay awake until they were undressed and tucked in bed.

Little Doc had gone to his room as soon as we came in. When I came downstairs again, Father had built the fire in the fireplace and taken *King Richard II* down from the mantelpiece. He was going to read to me. It had been almost a month since he had had a free evening for that.

The glow of the fire matched the glow of my feelings. I sat on my footstool and leaned my head against Father's knees. "It's been a beautiful day, hasn't it, Father. This is one of those days that I want to remember all my life—"

He turned the pages of the book. "Two people can have entirely different views of one day. It can be very beautiful for one. Someone else can look from another direction and see a very unhappy day."

"I think it was a happy day for everyone there today. Did you see Old Phineas' eyes? He loved it." I remembered the boy with the gun. "No. It wasn't a very happy day for Jeff Glazer."

"I have an idea that it wasn't a very happy day for the girls whose beaus danced with you all afternoon."

I laughed contentedly. "Oh, they didn't care. I had a wonderful time."

His voice was dry as the pages of the book still turned. "You look, the next time, and see if the belle of the ball doesn't dance with her head in the clouds, and her feet treading all over the toes of the wallflowers. There's a lot of sore toes back country tonight."

I turned on my stool and faced him. "Now, Father, you know that I wasn't deliberately taking anybody's 'beau' away from anybody there. And the minister asked me to be his partner—I didn't ask him!"

Father's eyes were on the book. "Mr. MacCreighton was a guest of honor, who asked 'Big Doc's gal' for the first dance because she was a sort of guest of honor, too."

I flushed. "Well, none of them there are anybody that I'd ever date. Not a single one of them."

"Then you were flirting."

"I was not. I was only having a good time."

His voice went on as if I had not spoken. "And a flirt always walks around with a halo of vanity around her head. By the way, do you remember what page we were on here? I forgot to mark the line."

My pride was hurt. Father had no right to scold me for this. "Father—I didn't do anything wrong."

"Ah, this is the line," he said. "The two buckets in the well. 'That bucket down and full of tears am I, drinking my griefs, whilst you mount up on high.'"

He settled deeper in his chair to read, and I turned back to my stool and faced the fire. Tears welled in my eyes; there was a tight lump in my throat. Father wasn't fair! I spent all my time working in the house, and he had taken one day that I wanted to always remember, and crumpled it like a piece of waste paper. He had made my popularity into something cold and common. They had all liked me—I hadn't tried to be a flirt. I wasn't like Nancy's cousin, Jinny Carter, from Little Rock, who had come to our

Senior party and monopolized all the boys, leaving the rest of us sitting smiling-faced and unhappy on the fringe. Jinny had all the money and clothes and liberties that the rest of us didn't have. And she had been from Little Rock—the boys had been flattered—

A cold thought came to me. Where was the difference? To the eyes of the back country, I was from the town, with clothes and a big house and a freedom that no girl there could ever hope for. I could play the piano, and was going to a school in a big city some day. I had everything. More than that, I was "Big Doc's gal." "Big Doc's gal" had come on their grounds and flaunted her weapons in their powerless faces. She had left them nothing to fight with.

A score of the day's pictures flashed like lantern slides before my eyes. The faces of the girls watching me from the benches—the shy, flattered eyes of the boys—the shrill laughter—my own flushed and happy being.

And Little Doc sitting with Father on the bench all afternoon. I had been cruel to Little Doc. We were always partners when we went to parties together—I had never left him before. I had forgotten him! Words that I had heard Mother say, once, long ago, came back to me in all their anger: "It makes me boil inside, Robert, to see Little Doc always stand aside for Sister. She's not worth it yet!" Mother was right: Little Doc had been apologizing to me when he opened the car door for me when we first arrived at Phineas Granther's, and I had been unkind.

I saw him now, standing under the apple tree during the wedding ceremony—his grin and wink of assurance when the gun was fired—the coat flung over his shoulders—his back and Father's, as they strode toward the car in the oak grove—

Suddenly I turned and gripped Father's knee. I had seen three other pictures: Little Doc's white face—the way he sat so still all afternoon—the way he had gone to his room as soon as we came in. "Father! Father—what happened to Little Doc today?"

He looked up from the book. In a moment he said, "He was shot."

"Shot—"

"Nothing serious. The bullet only grazed his shoulder a little. Nothing to upset the wedding day for."

My voice sounded from miles away. "No one knew—"

Father laughed his short, dry laugh. "You know how they all feel about Little Doc. I think Jeff Glazer would have been beaten to a pulp if any of the men had found out about it. Little Doc wouldn't let me say anything."

I had nothing to answer. Father went back to the reading.

"Father," I said thickly. "Don't read yet. I'm not finished."

He looked at me. It was hard to keep my eyes on his cold gray ones. Only my hold on his knee kept me there. Finally I said, "Father—" Oh, what did I want to say to him? "—is there any money left in the bank?"

"A little."

"I want to take lessons from Professor Howell." The words had come before I knew I had thought them. Father must understand!

"Sure he has anything to teach you?"

I flushed, but my eyes were steady on his. "Yes, sir. I don't know much of anything. I don't believe I know anything."

"All right. Call him up Monday and see about it." He looked back at the book again, then held it out to me. "You read a while. My throat's dry from all my yelling."

My hold relaxed on his knee. "You always go to sleep when I read."

"Well, there's no better music than Shakespeare to go to sleep by." I took the book and he leaned his head against the back of his chair. "It's down at the bottom of the page. 'Oh, that I were a mockery king of snow, Standing before the sun of Bolingbroke, To melt myself away in water drops!—'"

I turned back on the stool and found the place. "'Good King—Great King—and yet not greatly good—'" There was never any use in my trying to read to Father. He always went to sleep. He would be asleep before I went half a page farther. But what did it matter? The scene was almost finished. He wouldn't miss the last few paragraphs. "'—Then let him command a mirror hither straight, That it may show me what a face I have, Since it is bankrupt of its majesty . . .'"

# XII

IN NOVEMBER, THE "COALS TO NEWCASTLE" case broke in the Senate Chamber in the state capitol. Father presented his plan through the head of the State Board of Health, Dr. Simmons. Every last detail had been worked out in advance—the estimates, plans and legal details involved for a drainage ditch from Black Hollow down to the Arkansas River. Even Hudson Kaley was working with Father. He didn't dare not to: the water from Newcastle Lakes was draining into the swamp by no authority from the State Board of Health.

The bill was voted on in the Senate on the twenty-ninth of November.

Father came home for supper that night, his eyes red-rimmed and tired from another long day in the Senate gallery. The weeks and months of work and strain had begun to show on his face. There was something almost pathetic in his thin gray hair, his long, lanky frame. He was working too hard. The fight was hard for him.

He laughed at my worried look. "Dish up the victuals, Sister. I'll be all right when my stomach's fed."

"Tell me about the voting, first."

"Can't tell yet. Simmons said he would phone as soon as the votes come in."

"Then it will be finished?"

He laughed abruptly. "The battle hasn't half begun. Governor James still lurks in the Statehouse." He spat on his hands and rubbed them together. "He's an octopus with tentacles twelve feet long, but wait until I get started on him."

"You'll get him, Papa," Melie Kate said.

He reached over and pulled Melie and Ruth onto his knees. "Your Papa isn't licked yet," he said. "Come on and let's give the cook a ditty while she dishes up."

He stamped his feet on the floor, and the three voices sang after me as I went to the kitchen.

> "Jaybird sitting on a crooked limb,
>     I cocked my gun and I shot at him,
>     Said he 'Young man, don't you do thet agin'—"

Little Doc came in as we were eating.

"Here comes Old Curiosity," I said, as I unbolted the side door for him. "What do you bet he begged the whole evening off just to come home and get the news?"

Little Doc grinned. "It was your chicken dumplings, Madam. I could smell them clear up to Frank's."

"It's cornbread, not chicken dumplings. And we don't know what the Senate did. The votes haven't all been counted yet."

Little Doc straddled his chair without taking off his jacket. "Is that right?" he asked Father.

Father nodded. "Simmons said he'd call as soon as he found out. He hopes to find out tonight."

"How do you think it looked?"

Father chuckled. "Well, this morning the colored porter at the courthouse was betting six bits on my side, and this evening I heard him betting six bits on the other side. He's like a hound when the wind shifts."

"I bet Melie Kate a nickel," Ruth said.

"Except that you both bet on Father's side," I said. "You'll never make money that way."

Father spoke to Little Doc. "Are you off for the evening?"

"Frank said I could come home and celebrate."

"All right. You and Sister take Simmons' call if it comes. When I get back from hauling Sam Talbot's fever down, we'll see whether we toast with wine or gall."

A sound burst from my throat. "Father!"

He looked at me. They were all looking at me curiously. Had my voice been too loud? It seemed to me that the sound had been wrenched from me.

"Father—you're not going out tonight, are you?"

My voice had been normal again. Father turned back to his plate. "Can't afford to turn a man down when he's got no money and his fever's a hundred and five. Think of his pride."

"It's cold and you're tired," I said.

Father reached for a piece of cornbread. "You keep the fire roaring, and I'll be sitting in front of it by nine o'clock." He held up the piece of cornbread. "See this? Better than any piece of cake I've ever eaten." His tired eyes twinkled. "You're getting your mother's buttered thumb, Sister."

That was the night my Father died.

After he went out the front door, his overcoat flying wide open, his hat jammed low on his head, Little Doc and I stood by the living-room table, looking over the map of Black Hollow again. Melie Kate and Ruth were in the kitchen, washing the dishes.

After a few minutes, Little Doc looked up from the map and said, "Did you hear the car go, Sister?"

"No."

"Maybe he's having trouble getting it started. It's freezing cold."

He walked to the window and pulled the shade aside. For a long moment he stood there, looking out into the moonlit yard.

"See anything?" I said.

He let the shade fall in place. "I'll be back in a minute." He opened the front door and I heard his footsteps go across the porch and down the steps.

I looked down at the map again. The dishes were clattering in the kitchen, the fire crackled comfortably in the fireplace. Around me was the strange, cold feeling that I had known so many times before. Something was happening. Nothing that I could do now could stop it; nothing could ever stop it. It could only happen around me.

Little Doc came in again and stood with his back against the front door. "You'll have to help me, Sister," he said quietly. "Father's ill. He's had a heart attack."

"Yes," I said.

The door closed behind us, and we were down the yard to the car in the driveway. Father sat doubled up on the running-board, his head bent, his gaunt hands clutching his chest.

"Dr. White—" he gasped. "Get—White. Coronary—"

Little Doc's voice was calm. "I'll call him as soon as we *g*  you indoors. Help me on the other side, Sister."

The instant that I touched Father's shoulder, a shudder went over him. He looked up at me and tried to laugh. An arrow went through my throat. I read his face there in the moonlight; the look in his eyes, the sweat and the agony. I had never read it before, but I knew it now.

Little Doc's sharp order brought me back, and the long struggle to the house began.

Little Doc's strength was superhuman. I only seemed to follow him. Up the slope of the yard, with every frozen blade of dry grass etched in shadow, up the three steps, across the porch, into the living-room.

Father leaned against the wall, sweat dripping from his face. The dishes still clattered in the kitchen. Melie Kate and Ruth were laughing and talking.

"Upstairs—" Father's voice said. "Bed—"

"Don't you think you'd better stay here on the sofa?" Little Doc said.

Father's lips were all the suffering ever known. "Upstairs," he said again. "Keep—girls—away."

His arms were dead weights around our shoulders. Every breath was a gasp of agony, but he made us go on and on, up the stairs. I saw every long step of torture as we went up. The stair with the crack, dust in the corners—I had never been a good cleaner—the woodwork that needed polishing again, up and up, the weight that was crushing me to earth, the stairs that never ceased.

Then Little Doc pushed the bedroom door open with his foot, and in another eon we had Father on the bed. I reached over and put my hand on his wet forehead. His big rough hand was too weak to come to me, so I put my other hand in his. His words still came in tortured gasps. "Stay—with girls. Get—Myrtle—"

Little Doc took my hand from Father's. "You call Dr. White when you go downstairs, Sister. I'll stay here."

The quietness of his voice was a rock that steadied the house. It reached out and touched me, too. "I'll take care of everything downstairs," I said. "Everything's all right, Father."

An hour of eternity passed. Dr. White came, and then there was no sound from upstairs. Words drummed over and over in my head. "Keep— girls—away." I had heard the words before. The woman on the living-room table, "Don't worry, Miz Doc—we won't wake your little ones." Here is the man and the back country, sired in one, dust of dust, flesh of flesh. Silent in the agony of life and death.

Melie Kate and Ruth came in when they were finished in the kitchen, and took their schoolbooks from the table.

The firelight and the lamp on the table made the only light in the room. Melie Kate studied at the table, her head bent over arithmetic problems. Ruth sat cross-legged at my feet, her head leaning against my knees as she read her reading lesson over and over.

I heard Little Doc come down the stairs. He stopped at the foot of the staircase.

"The black cow chased Step Hen—" Ruth's voice said in my consciousness.

"Stephen, Ruth," I corrected.

"The black cow chased Stephen—"

Suddenly I became aware that Little Doc still stood at the staircase. A pounding flame roared through me and I turned to him with an effort. His tall form stood silent. He nodded only once. A world crashed to bits. My eyes followed him as he walked across the floor and into the dining-room. The door closed softly and my thoughts were left behind.

My thoughts! How does one begin thinking again when suddenly the very essence of one's life has been dissolved? Laughter in the house—the pivot of the day—a gaunt, bony finger pointing to Arcturus, "There's millions of stars up there, Sister, but you can only have one—" "I only want one, Father." Evenings before the fire. "What could we read tonight, Father?" "Let's try Shelley. 'Adonais.' " That horrible line "— and cold hopes swarm like worms within our living clay—" "Oh, Father, don't make me read that line again. It has the feeling of putty—lifeless, encasing putty."

Those hours of reading were finished. Death, with a touch of his blasting finger had erased all pages of books.

I sat unmoving—a clear, cold feeling around me. I looked down from a high ground—aware of no thoughts, only sensory touches to my being. The dry crackling of the flames. The drone of Ruthie's voice. The weight of her head against my knees. The soft markings of Melie Kate's pencil with the chewed eraser. A rain crow mourning in the woods. The shouting stillness of the Presence upstairs. The dirge of the dialing phone in the other room.

Two thoughts entered slowly and heavily. Melie Kate and Ruth. One can live with Aunt Melicent, the other with Uncle Eldon. Six months before Mother could get home—maybe longer. Uncle Eldon, with his quick intellect, must understand that Ruth's stolid ways of thinking take patient thoughtfulness. Aunt Melicent mustn't guide Melie Kate's artistic fingers too much; her shyness is like a sensitive plant. Little Doc and I can decide later where we can go.

Melie Kate yawned and stretched like a cat. Ruth's voice paused in mid-sentence as she turned a page. "Ruthie—" My voice was cracked and dry. "Ruthie—sit here by me. The light's bad there."

Early in the dawn of the next morning the wagons began arriving. The first one creaked beneath my bedroom window in the last shadows of the night. It stopped in the road outside. Hushed voices blended with the crunch of footsteps on the frozen ground and the leathery clink of the horses' harness. Farmers taking produce to the town curb markets, I thought. They often stopped to water their horses from the trough by the big oak tree.

The stars were still out when the second wagon groaned into the yard. Footsteps stamped on the crusted ground and up the steps of the front porch. A door opened, and the footsteps muffled into the house.

Strange! I walked to my bedroom door and to the top of the stairs. A cadence of whispering voices came from below. Busy voices. A head came around the corner of the staircase and seeing me, the rest of the body followed. Fat old Fräulein from across the road. "Ah, Miss Mary, there's dust a-laying in this house. It can't be here when the doctor gets back. Tell me where the cloths be."

"In the pantry," I answered. "Who else is there?"

"Come down for yourself if you can't be sleeping. They're people from back country."

People from back country! Ten and twenty miles back country! Four hours' ride in their creaky wagons—and they were here in the dawn. What grapevine had sent the news of the death of their doctor so quickly?

I knocked on Little Doc's door. No answer. He must be downstairs with Fräulein and the hushed voices. I hadn't undressed; back to my room for shoes and a sweater and I was downstairs, too. I stood by the staircase, the same place that Little Doc had stood the evening before.

Fräulein had found the dustcloths; she was in every corner at once, dust flying from the whirling cloth in her hands. Little Doc stood by a great bearded man at the front door. Jake Granther from Granite Hill. His heavy mackintosh hung shapeless from his shoulders, and his boots were wrinkled and smelling of oil.

"I heerd about Big Doc," he said, his enormous hands twisting his stained hat. "We brung turnips." I held out my hand. He crossed to me in two great strides.

"I'll get you a spade," Little Doc said. "You can bury them in the back yard if the ground is loose enough."

They went through the door toward the kitchen, Little Doc's tall lankiness coming only to the huge farmer's shoulder.

Two women sat by the fireplace. "I'm Hank Jarvis's wife," one said. I remembered. Hank Jarvis worked on the railroad. "Hank blowed the whistle three times when the train come by tonight, and we knowed somethin' warn't right at Big Doc's house. Berta and me thought ye'd be needin' someone to do the cookin'.' "

"It's kind of you. There's no bread."

"We brung bread," Berta said. "Eggs, too."

By ten o'clock that morning the yard was full of wagons and battered trucks from back country. People from the town hadn't arrived yet. It was too early.

The sun shone gloriously and warm. Horses stamped and whinnied in the woods where they were tied. Indoors, the atmosphere was charged with the bustle of busy people. A warm odor of fresh bread came from the kitchen. Omie darned socks in the dining-room. "I found these in the basket on the sewing machine," she said reprovingly, a finger through a hole in the toe. "Little Doc's, too."

A young girl with old-woman eyes pushed a plump baby toward me. "This is Mary Kate Ruth."

Mary Kate Ruth, named for the three daughters of the doctor who had taken the young mother into his house one night when a hospital couldn't be reached in time. The baby that had been delivered on the long oak table in the living-room. "She didn't make a single cry, Sister," Little Doc had said to me afterwards. "She looked up at Mother and said, 'Don't worry, Miz Doc, we won't wake your babies.' " Yes, the living-room table still bore the deep scratches made by those anguished fingernails.

I turned away and stood in the doorway to the living-room. Around the fireplace were the men from back country. Their pipes were lit. "See this thumb? Thar's where the buzz saw went clean through it. Big Doc stuck it back on and danged if they didn't grow smack together agin'." The thumb reached down with a forefinger and struck a match on the brick fireplace. A haze of smoke spiraled toward the ceiling.

"It's mighty funny," said a gaunt man with a black beard. "I always thought if Doc ever died it'd be of pneumonia. He never buttoned thet overcoat of his'n. Never wore no gloves, neither. Wife'd say, 'Git in here, Doc, and stick them hands in this hot water.' Doc'd laugh and say, 'Now, tush, Miz Barrington, you know I cain't breathe when my hands got gloves on 'em. They cain't feel,' he'd say. 'Might as well be dead hands.' "

Jake Granther propped a booted foot on an andiron. "When Doc gouged a bullet out'n thet laig he larned me a poem." He spat thoughtfully into the fire. "Mighty educated man Big Doc was. Poem went, 'Tobaccy is a dirty weed. I like it. It makes you thin, It makes you lean, It takes the hair plumb off yore bean, It's the worst damned stuff I've ever seen. I like it.' "

Omie brushed past me toward the men at the fireplace. "Up, Jake. Big Doc's comin' home."

Jake's foot came off the andiron and he looked toward the window. A long black car was driving into the yard. The men rose and turned toward the door. The man with the scarred thumb knocked his pipe against the mantelpiece.

A song soared upward. A song in my heart. No song of grief; a song of love. Love for a roaring train that plowed through the night trumpeting to the countryside that Big Doc, with his rough kind hands wouldn't be knocking at their doors any longer. Love for an inarticulate man, whose sympathy lay in turnips buried in the frost of the back yard. Love for Fräulein's hands that brushed away the dust; for long scratches on a table; for bread and eggs in the kitchen. Where was the problem that had weighted down my heart? There was no problem. Miz Doc had released us first—now Big Doc. Released the four of us to find a piece of life together. The four of us were one.

Melie Kate stood in the doorway with me. Ruth touched my sleeve. "Aunt Melicent's car is coming up," she said, close to me. "Sister— wherever you're going, I'm going too." The words of the eternal Ruth. I couldn't see her; a fog was between us. I could only hear Little Doc's voice in the distance, speaking the words for me. "Yes, Ruthie. No one's going anywhere. We're staying here."

# XIII

IT GETS DARK early in November. When Bill drove us home from the cemetery the next afternoon, the clock said only five o'clock, but the sky was already gray and cold. Dead leaves scratched across the porch in a sudden gust of wind. The sun was gone.

Lights burned brightly in the house, however. Fraulein must have left only a moment before—the fire crackled merrily in the fireplace, the dining-room table was set for supper.

Bill came in just long enough to put another log on the fire, and warm his hands before he drove to the airport.

"I wish I could stay longer," he said, brushing the wood lint from his hands. "The seven o'clock plane is the last one back tonight."

"Do you operate or something in the morning?"

He grinned—a grin oddly out of place in his white, strained face. "Nope. Only a consultation with a rich old guy from Kansas City—but a rich old guy who might lay a golden egg if I handle it right."

"Don't worry about us, Bill. We'll be all right here tonight. Little Doc gets back tomorrow." Little Doc had driven to Booneville to be with Mother. "It's not long until Christmas now. We'll see you then."

"I'll climb down the chimney with Santa Claus."

He tipped my chin high with one hand, grinned again, and then was gone. When the last sound of the car had died away, I called Melie Kate and Ruth to come downstairs to supper.

I put them to bed by seven o'clock that night. The day had been tiring for both of them. I came back downstairs, built the fire until it roared and crackled, and sat at the piano to play awhile. The house was too silent with no music.

After one page of the Beethoven, I stopped—all the chords were empty, toneless shells that fell coldly in the big space of the room. It would be better to read. Words could fill the room more easily than music tonight.

But then, it wasn't easy to find a book to read, either, for the bookcases were full of ghosts. The bookcase on the right of the fireplace had Father's books: Goethe's letters to Bettina, that we had read only last spring; *The Old Curiosity Shop,* that was the only one of Dickens' books which none of us had read. "We'll leave that one," Father had laughed one night. "Then when we're old and the devil comes for us, we can say, 'Oh, no, sir, you'll have to wait awhile for me. I haven't finished all of Dickens.' " And there was the old gray Latin primer that Little Doc had had his first Latin lessons from. Father had found it in a second-hand shop on Washington Avenue, and had mended the broken back with strips of adhesive plaster. I could hear Little Doc's five-year-old voice as he stood between Father's knees and repeated the words after Father.

"Puer . . . boy."

"Puer . . . boy."

"Puella . . . girl."

"Puella . . . girl."

I left that bookcase and went to the one by the foot of the staircase, where Mother's books were kept. I took *The Prophet* from the second shelf and pulled my footstool before the fire.

It was no use. The words that were vibrant, living words when Mother read them, were empty, socketless eyes tonight. I could see far through them, back to the cold windy hill of the afternoon, the faces of the people, the deep tones of the minister's voice, the muted footsteps of the people who walked in front and in back of us when we left the cemetery to come home. I could see far through to Mother's heart, that was torn from her body and wept in her chair by the fire tonight.

I laid the book down, and stood with my back to the fireplace, facing the two gaunt chairs. No words, no music in the room tonight. For the first time since the house was built, there was nothing in the living-room. The silence rang and droned in my ears—it swelled and modulated, grew louder and louder—there wasn't anything in the room to hear. Nothing.

A knock came on the front door, but I still stood frozen. The palms of my hands were wet with perspiration.

The knock came again. A wild thought penetrated. Bill! Bill had come back! He had come back so that I wouldn't be alone this evening!

"Oh, Bill!" I cried out to him.

I flung the front door wide open and stood there. The man silhouetted against the street light wasn't Bill. It was the minister from back country. Mr. MacCreighton. When I stood there, saying nothing, he held out a box and said, "It's a coconut cake. Mrs. Toon forgot to leave it for Little Doc today."

The wind blew in, cold through the open door. I unhooked the screen and stepped back into the living-room. "Come in, Mr. MacCreighton."

He stood awkward and ill at ease while I closed the door and took the box from him. "Thank you for coming all the way back," I said. "Mrs. Toon would have spent all night wringing her hands for forgetting it."

He grinned wryly. "She had practically wrung Tod's neck off for forgetting to remind her about it, by the time I reached their house. He lent me his truck to bring it back in."

He put his coat on the long oak table, and turned toward the fireplace. I set the box on the table. "It's been a cold trip back. If you'll sit down I'll get you some coffee."

"Only a little," he said. "But black as a hottentot."

When the percolator was on, and I came back to the living-room, Mr. MacCreighton sat in Father's big chair. A swift feeling came to me—but an odd feeling. More a breath of released tension than a hurt: Father's chair was filled.

I sat in Mother's chair. Mr. MacCreighton pulled a pipe from his pocket and motioned toward the fire. "Too bad there's not a cricket to go with the hearth and the pipe."

"There was a cricket one summer. A little green one. Melie Kate and Ruth caught him out in the field and Little Doc named him Archibald."

"Is he hibernating?"

"No. Mother deposed him. She said his top notes were flat so she swept him out one day." I watched the hands with the bony wrists, as they packed the tobacco in the pipe. There was something easing in the slow manner and speech of this man. "Father wouldn't bring Mother an apple for a week after that," I continued. "He always brought her an apple when he had a good day, and he'd put it up there on the mantel for her to find." I chuckled. "Only he always ate it himself."

The minister put the pipe in his mouth and reached in his pocket for a match. "My father was a funny one, too. Any time there was company that Mother was right proud of, he'd haul out an old frayed piece of rope and tell how he had cut Uncle Zack down from the tree, himself." His hands cradled the pipe and a pungent odor of pipe smoke came into the room.

"Your father sounds like mine," I said. "Father had four degrees, and he would argue with anybody that people go to college too much. He wrote an article that was published in the newspaper once, and it was terrible. He said that boys come home from college knowing how to say 'Polly wants a cracker' in fourteen different languages, without having been taught how to reach out and grab the cracker in one language. I don't wonder that a lot of people used to laugh at his funny ideas."

Mr. MacCreighton leaned back in the chair and stretched his long legs out before him. "There were probably a lot laughing with him, too, though. There's a big difference."

"He never cared." I settled deeper in Mother's chair. "I wish you could have read the article he wrote about our family tree, too. People in Little Rock were tracing their ancestry back and getting it put in the paper, so he wrote about ours." I had to laugh, remembering it. "Even Mother had to laugh at Aunt Josie."

"What about Aunt Josie?"

"Aunt Josie couldn't read. He told how she'd borrow books and keep them a week or so, and then take them back and tell how much she had enjoyed them. She had the Clayborne pride—she wouldn't let anybody know she'd never learned to read or write." I laughed again—funny how the story was still so amusing to me when I had heard it over and over again. "Only once she borrowed a Bible." I stopped to get my breath, and Mr. MacCreighton was already chuckling with me. "When she took it back and the woman who had lent it said, 'How did you like it, Josie?' Aunt Josie said, 'Oh, it was all right, I reckon. Only it ended like all the rest of them—the boy and girl got married.' "

I leaned back in my chair, laughing until the tears were in my eyes, and Mr. MacCreighton guffawed until the room rang. I sat up and reached for my handkerchief, but someway I couldn't stop laughing.

Suddenly Mr. MacCreighton was up from his chair and striding toward the kitchen.

"Oh, my heavens!" I cried. "The coffee. I forgot it!"

I ran after him, my laughter stopped now. By the time I reached the stove he had already turned the fire off under the sputtering pot. I stood looking at the brown streaks running in sizzling lines down the sides.

"What in the world is wrong with the thing?" I said.

He reached for the pot-holder on the hook on the wall, and carried the pot to the sink. "Maybe you'd better let me make the next cup," he said. "I'll stay here and keep an eye on it."

"Then I'll get Effie Toon's cake and cut it. Little Doc won't care and Effie won't ever know."

I ran back to the living-room for the cake. The moment I came in from the dining-room, I knew that the room was different now. I could almost hear a song through it again. Something had put voices and laughter in it again.

Laughter!

What must the minister think of me? I had sat in Mother's chair, and laughed at Father's jokes until my sides ached and I was limp all over. He had laughed, too, but he had only been covering it for me.

I walked back to the kitchen and set the cake box on the table. "I don't know why I did that," I said to him. "I don't know why I laughed like that."

He measured the water carefully into the pot and set it on the stove before he answered. Then he took the little mirror from over the sink and held it up before me. He had gray eyes, too, and they looked down on me as Father's had looked so many times.

"Look in here," he said.

I looked in the mirror. Tear streaks ran down my cheeks. My eyes were swollen—too bright and swollen for laughter.

"Sometimes it all means the same thing," he said. He turned and hung the mirror back over the sink. Standing there by the table, I suddenly felt exhausted and tired. No other feeling. All the cold emptiness of an hour before was gone.

Mr. MacCreighton grinned and motioned toward the box. "Better get to work on that cake. Won't be long before this pot of coffee is ready to be poured."

"You know," I said, opening the table drawer for a knife. "For some reason I haven't wanted to cry at all. There's been nothing to cry about." I opened the lid of the box and took the cake out. "When I've thought about anything, I've caught myself wondering who is going to finish the job that Father didn't get to finish."

Mr. MacCreighton didn't answer.

"That drainage ditch from Black Hollow meant more to him than anything he's ever done," I said. "He fought with everything he had to fight with—and he wasn't a fighter. It hurts horribly to think that he let himself be killed doing the thing in life he hated most, and that maybe there won't be anybody to finish it for him."

Mr. MacCreighton said, "I've read about Black Hollow."

I laid two pieces of cake on the saucers, and put the big cake back in the box. "I don't believe any of the men who were working with him will go ahead with it now. He'd had to push it down their throats to get it before the Senate. Dr. Simmons was to call the night—night before last, but he didn't call. He won't do it now."

Mr. MacCreighton took the bubbling pot from the stove, and I picked up the tray with the cake and cups and saucers. We went back to the living-room. Mr. MacCreighton pulled the two chairs closer to the fire while I cleared one of the little tables of its books and papers, and set it between the chairs. Then we sat down and Mr. MacCreighton picked up the coffeepot.

"Here's to a cricket named Archibald," he said.

"Why?"

"Because it sounds poetic, nothing else." He reached across and poured my cup first. One startled look into the steaming cup and we both sat back in our chairs and laughed again until the room rang. Mr. MacCreighton had forgotten to put the coffee in the pot: we had boiling water to toast Archibald with.

# XIV

WE WERE ALL at breakfast, two days later, when the trucks and cars again rolled in from back country. Little Doc was trying to persuade Ruth to eat her oatmeal, so we paid no attention to the first Ford that passed. Then a truck lumbered by, a second, a third.

"That sounds strange," I said. "Are they going to curb market en masse, this morning?"

Little Doc got up from the table and went to look out the side door. "This isn't curb-market day. This is Friday."

Two more cars rattled by. There was something oddly disturbing in the steady roll of wheels. Cull Brant passed, bent over the wheel of his truck. He looked in as he went by and raised a hand in greeting. Little Doc raised his hand in return. Cull turned back and the car went on.

"There's no produce in their cars, anyway," I said. "Something seems to be going on."

"I don't know what it is but I'm going to find out." Little Doc turned from the door and went to the closet under the stairs for his leather jacket.

"Just a minute—" I said. "It's eight o'clock now. You'll be late for school."

"School can wait." The side door slammed behind him.

"Can we stay home, too, Sister?" Ruth asked.

"You finish your oatmeal and trot right on. They're probably all trekking to town for clothes or something. Little Doc just imagines something is wrong."

I bundled them up for school when the oatmeal dishes were empty, and stood at the side door to watch after them as they walked up to Main Street. Their road led straight down Maple Street, so the caravan of cars wouldn't disturb them. The cars were turning at our house, going the two blocks to Main Street, then turning down toward town. Something was surely wrong—Little Doc wasn't imagining things.

He came running up the side steps in another moment. His eyes were bright with excitement. "I've just seen Otho Granther. You'll never guess what's happened, Sister. They're headed for Governor James' office!"

"What's happened, Little Doc?"

He laughed. "Nothing's happened. We're going to make it happen."

"What do you mean by 'we'?"

He picked up his gloves from the windowseat and pulled them on. "I'm going, too. I'm going in with Otho. The minute something happens I'll telephone you." The door was closing behind him again and I had to run to catch him before he was gone.

"You didn't tell me what it was, Little Doc!"

"We're getting Black Hollow drained!" he called back from the edge of the yard.

Black Hollow drained! That was the sound in the long line of wheels rolling to the Statehouse to see the Governor! Father's dream was going to the Statehouse for him!

I was so excited that I wanted to shout. I watched Little Doc swing himself over the unopened car door of Otho Granther's Ford, and turn to wave as the car edged back into line and started on toward Main Street. Oh, if only I could go, too! Down at Main Street, curious people were already lining the sidewalk. The first car must be almost at the bridge that crossed the river to Little Rock by now.

I looked down the road to see the rest of the line that was coming. There were wagons, too, now. And there was one woman going! Omie! She waved from the passing wagon and frantically I waved back. She yelled something, but I couldn't hear, and then she pointed back down the line. In another moment Jake Granther's wagon hove into sight—behind it was young Jed Granther's car, and in it, Old Phineas, the old, old man of the hills, bundled up until he was a mummy so still in the seat. His wrinkled old face turned and looked in at me at the door as he passed. The patriarch with his tents had come to move the mountain. If only Father could have seen! A mist blurred the glass pane.

The line rolled by for almost an hour. Silence lay heavily on the air after the last wagon had turned at Main Street and disappeared past the row of houses. I turned then from the door: I would know no more until Little Doc came back.

He didn't return until after dark that evening. Cars and trucks had started back down the road by five o'clock, but he was in one of the last cars to come down.

His eyes were still bright with excitement, but his face was flushed and tired. He hadn't much to tell. John MacCreighton, the minister, had started the whole long journey—Phineas Granther had done the talking.

Old Phineas had been in the Governor's office for long over an hour. Tom Harding Hammond, the lawyer, had stalked in with his briefcase around three o'clock, and then Old Phineas had come out, wrapped himself in his blankets again and the journey home had started.

But the headlines in the *Gazette* that he had, told the rest of the story. Father's map of Black Hollow was on the front page—his own funny drawing with the huge mosquitoes perched on dead stumps, larvae that swam merrily among cattails and green slime.

By Sunday, Father's work was done. The paper had the whole story, this time. The bill had been passed by the Senate, Governor James had added his signature, and in the spring, Black Hollow was to be drained and filled in.

The question of finances had to come up in our family of four now.

Tom Harding Hammond came with his briefcase, one evening in December, and Little Doc and I sat in the library with him, at Father's desk. Mr. Hammond adjusted his thick glasses carefully; slowly arranged the papers from his briefcase on the desk.

"There isn't much money," he said, finally. He never had extra words. "There was no insurance, you know—your father didn't believe in it. There was a postal savings account of some seven hundred dollars, however." He shifted the pages of papers. "With the clearance of the funeral cost, and the remainder of Mrs. Clayborne's stay at Booneville, there is around two hundred dollars left. There are no other debts—your father didn't believe in debts, either. The house has no mortgage and no back taxes due." He held up a small piece of paper. "The only debit is an electric bill for two dollars and seventeen cents."

He reached in the briefcase and pulled out another paper, a long, typewritten sheet. "A few days ago, a man came to me from a place back country, called Mount Horeb. An old man had sent orders—" He was dry and austere. "—Orders," he repeated, as if we were responsible, "to bring me out to discuss a legal matter. It seems that there was money still owed to your father by several families around Mount Horeb"—the name sounded so unfamiliar on his tongue—"and several other neighboring settlements. He dictated this to me." He handed me the long sheet. "You two are to give your signed approval, or any alternative that you wish. Those were my orders." I could almost have sworn that there was ironic humor in his dry voice.

Little Doc and I read the sheet together.

"There is money owed Big Doctor Clayborne for doctoring. We ask to pay it this way:

Eskar Toler:     One bushel potatoes each, December, March, June.
John Whistler:   Six dollars owed for pneumonia. Butter and cheese on going to the curb market.
Jake Granther:   Onions, half a hog. Cash when cotton picking starts.
Ez Whitecotton: Twenty cans canned vegetables. Twenty jars jelly and preserves."

The list went on and on. It covered the whole long page. Phineas Granther, High Lama of the back country! The patriarch who watches his flock.

"I've checked it with the books. The amounts haven't varied more than a few cents for medicine in a case or so." Tom Harding Hammond's voice seemed far away. He cleared his throat. "I can't promise you much for collections in the town. When a physician is deceased, the debts decease with him. The majority seem to feel under no obligation to pay."

# XV

CHRISTMAS EVE, AND the pine tree stood in the corner by the staircase, its topmost branch touching the ceiling. We had gone to the woods for it the day before. The room was filled with the pungent green smell of pine, the crackling of the fire, the awareness of cold and snow outdoors.

Melie Kate was upstairs, wrapping her presents. Ruthie sat in Father's chair before the fire, chuckling to herself over the new book that someone at school had given her.

I came in the room to pull the shades down. "What's so funny, Ruth?"

"Just a funny picture."

She went on a few pages, then turned back to the first one and chuckled softly again.

"Come on, Ruthie, let me see!" I reached over her shoulder and pinioned the book down before she could close it. Under a picture of a country mouse, piteous and scrawny, moth-eaten whiskers, she had printed "Mary." Under the city mouse, plump and smug, a fatuous grin under its waxed mustache, she had printed, "Biull."

"Ruth! Such spelling! And in your new book."

Her eyes danced mischievously. "It looks just like him, Sister."

"Well, it doesn't look like me. Erase it and don't ever write in your books again."

I saw the page erased, and Ruth's short pigtails disappear around the landing to go upstairs to help Melie Kate. I pulled the rest of the shades down and went back to the kitchen to finish the supper dishes. We had been eating at the kitchen table lately; the dining-room table was too big for only four of us.

I had hardly begun on the dishes again, when Little Doc's footsteps crunched up the path from the road. He was early. I wiped my hands on my apron and unbolted the side door to let him in.

"You're early, Little Doc."

He stamped the snow from his clothes and stepped inside. "Frank let me off for Christmas Eve. Business isn't so good tonight, anyway." He handed me the box of candy under his arm. "Frank sent it."

"Five pounds again! He never misses a Christmas."

I went back to the dishes. Little Doc hung his leather jacket on the peg by the stove, and sat at the table.

"Haven't you eaten?" I asked.

"Yes, I ate at Frank's. I just want a bite." He spread a piece of corn-bread with muscadine jelly and poured himself a glass of milk. "Did you hear from the sanitarium?"

I nodded. "Dr. Shipton's letter came in the afternoon mail. I put it on your desk. He said that the hemorrhage wasn't dangerous and that X-ray shows no spread of infection, but he thinks she must have a period of complete rest, anyway. That means we don't go up to see her tomorrow."

"Did he say what caused the hemorrhage?"

"No. Only an unfortunate incident which happens occasionally, he said. I don't understand all his technical words—you'll have to read those yourself." Later, I added, "Bill's not going to be able to come tomorrow, either. Another emergency consultation in the morning."

Little Doc laughed the short dry laugh that was so like Father's now. "That means I get both drumsticks, anyway." He poured more milk in his glass. "Where are Melie Kate and Ruth?"

"Upstairs wrapping presents." Remembering something, I laughed, too. "You know the half dollar you gave them each to do their shopping with?"

"Yes."

"Ruthie got everybody a present—nine of us, counting all the aunts and uncles—and only spent nine cents. She got Christmas cards. She brought me the forty-one cents and said it was to use for groceries." Suddenly her outstretched mitten with the nickels and pennies had become a coffer full to the brim with golden coins. She had made us rich this Christmas.

Little Doc's plate clinked as he laid his knife across it. "I had a good offer for a job yesterday," he said. "A guy who's opening a new sandwich shop over the river, came in Frank's and said he could use me if I'd work full time. I told him I'd take it if he'd wait until exams are over next month."

I looked at him. "You aren't serious?"

"Yes, I am. I was going to quit school at mid-term and work a while, anyway. We need money."

"Not that badly."

"That's what you think." He came over and slid his plate and glass into the dishwater. "We don't know what's going to happen next. Might be eating shoe leather by next Christmas."

"Then it's time to think about it six months from now." My voice was sharp. "I won't have you doing such a silly thing, Little Doc—stopping school just four months before you graduate!"

There was a long moment before he spoke. His voice was quiet. "I do what I think best, Sister. Next September, if things are all right, I'll go back and finish at mid-term."

I saw his firm, hard face—the level gray eyes.

"I'm sorry," I said. "I didn't mean to get angry. I couldn't stand to see a year lost that way. Next September you were going to start your—" My voice trailed off. Start what? Pre-Med? On what? "I'm sorry," I said again.

He turned and went on through the door.

Then, suddenly, I ran after him. "Little Doc! Wait a minute!" I reached him at the door into the living-room. "Little Doc—please—" My hands were soapy on his shirt-sleeves. "You can't stop school now, Little Doc! You mustn't!" Oh, he must hear what I knew so well. "If you aren't finished with school this June, and next September the chance is waiting for you to start your pre-med work, it might never come again if you aren't ready to take it. You have to be ready when your time comes! We can get along here all right!" He wasn't understanding me! "Oh, Little Doc, listen to me! A long, long time ago we started some place together. Nothing was ever going to stop us—remember? No matter what happened, we were still going to keep our ship heading straight—" My hands were a steel grip on his arms. "Little Doc, please don't leave me now!"

His face hadn't changed. His gray eyes went straight through me. He took my hands from his arms, and turned and went through the living-room, upstairs.

I stood there until the door closed to his room. Then I went back to the kitchen. I finished the dishes, set the table for breakfast, and then took my coat from the closet under the stairs and went out on the front porch. I sat on the swing, my feet up before me as I used to sit when Father was there with me.

The sting of the cold air felt good on my face. The sky was black, with silver stars. They waved and twinkled above the snow. Arcturus was up there somewhere—no need to look for it. It had long ago been swallowed up in the winter sky. I leaned my head against the swing, and closed my eyes, and all the bitter tears came. Those bitter tears that I had thought were locked away so safely. They all came—down to the last dregs.

I don't know how long I sat there. My lips had tasted of salt forever when the screen door opened and Little Doc came and sat beside me.

"Don't cry, Sister," he said. "I needed a good poke to remind me, I guess. I kept thinking of you stopping your music lessons and not saying anything about it—" His hand was awkward on my shoulder. "Stop crying now, Sister. I'm still here."

I wanted to speak to him, but I couldn't just then.

"Oh, I don't know what to do when a girl cries," he said, disgustedly. "If I were like Father, I could say that poem that Mother used to say to you—I don't know anything about poetry."

I straightened. "Everything's all right, Little Doc. I don't believe all my pretty words any more, either."

I put my feet down to the porch floor. How tired I was! My back ached, my body was exhausted and numb with cold. "That poem that you were talking about is by James Whitcomb Riley," I said. I could hear Mother saying it—

> "There, Little Girl, don't cry—
> They have broken your doll, I know.
> And your tea-set blue,
> And your doll-house, too—
> But they're things of the long ago. . . ."

Empty words, with no comfort any more. Now it was Christmas Eve, the snow was hard and crisp, candles were lit in Fräulein's house across the road. Somewhere carolers were singing, "Oh, Little Town of Bethlehem, How Still We See Thee Lie—" It was too early in the evening for carolers. But the words came, clear and close:

> "Yet in thy dark streets shineth
> The everlasting light—"

"That's right here," Little Doc said, suddenly. "They're at the side of the house."

He left the swing and walked to the end of the porch. He motioned to me. "Come here, Sister."

I went over and stood beside him. He pushed the clematis vine a little to one side for me to see better. At the side steps stood dark figures against the snow—six of them—one, the leader, standing taller and a bit apart from the others.

"They're from back country!" I whispered. That tall figure was the minister, John MacCreighton.

How far they had come! In the woods across the road, the horses stamped and snorted softly in the cold wintry air.

A warm, tingling glow crept along my veins. "They've come to stay a while," I whispered again. "There's doughnuts and apple cider in the house. I'll go fix it. You stay here and ask them in when they've finished."

I turned. The voices had begun another song.

"Silent Night, Holy Night,
All is calm—all is bright—"

"Oh, Little Doc," I said, almost laughing. "Look at that! I've forgotten to light the candle for the Christ Child!"

# XVI

By the middle of January, Mother had almost recovered from the hemorrhage, and Dr. Shipton let me go to Booneville to see her. Little Doc drove me to the station to catch the early morning train.

Mother was sitting in the glass-enclosed porch of the infirmary when I arrived that afternoon. It was difficult to believe that she had been ill. Her skin was tanned and rosy; her eyes as snapping black as ever.

"I should look well," she said, when I laughed about it. "I sit here, hogging the sunshine all day long. I've grown into the most useless individual that ever lived."

"We'll put you to work when you get home," I said. "Little Doc says he's going to buy you a plow."

"To plow what?"

"Well, Mr. Johnson came down the other day and said we could use his field if we wanted to put in a garden. He must think we're starving to death in that big house."

Mother settled deeper in her blankets. "There is the place for you to begin talking," she said. "I want to hear everything's that's happened since—" she hesitated, "—Christmas."

I was glad that there was only good news to tell. I showed her the list that Old Phineas had sent in from back country. I told her about Melie Kate and Ruth's schoolwork, Little Doc's job at Frank's, the practicing that I still found time to get done. Nonetheless, I was more and more relieved as the hands of the clock dissolved the hour to stay, and no mention had been made of Father. When there were only ten minutes of the hour left, and we sat for a moment with nothing else to talk about, I began to grow panicky. I searched quickly for another incident to tell. I almost blurted out the first one that came to my mind.

"I have one problem, Mother. It's Melie Kate." My words seemed to hang in air: I could have bitten my tongue off. I had never intended to speak of that—it would work itself out. Now Mother would worry.

But Mother only nodded her head. "I've been expecting to hear that for some time."

"She isn't disobedient or naughty," I added, hastily. "She's—oh, it's nothing important, I suppose. I think she misses you too much."

Mother's face was thoughtful. "Don't forget that Melie Kate and Ruth are two entirely different people to handle. Ruth's a grin and a chuckle—she always has been. Melie Kate is a lot like you."

"That doesn't help me one bit. I understand Ruth much more than I do Melie Kate."

Mother laughed. "Of course you do." She settled deeper in her chair and looked out the windows. "This looks like a good chance to find out what sort of teacher you can make, Sister."

I opened my mouth to speak, but her face was turned away and her voice went on. "There's just one thing to remember—a teacher is always the same whether she's in a schoolroom, or seated at a piano, or just a mother." She laughed to herself. "That's a funny one. 'Just a mother.' " She must have been waiting for me to say something, but when I didn't, she breathed deeply of the warm air and her eyes twinkled. "I wish you would look at that mountain over there. It worried me for a long time until I discovered that it was because the ridge down the side looked just like Uncle Jonathan's nose. I never did particularly like Uncle Jonathan."

A nurse came into the room, padding like a cat in her rubber-soled shoes. It was time for me to leave. I had found no answer to my question about Melie Kate, but I had discovered one big thing. Mother wasn't worried about us. She was getting well, and she knew that Little Doc and I could do our job until she came home.

I walked out of the sanitarium and down the road to the town and the railroad station, on the lightest feet that I had known since Father had died.

# XVII

IT WAS 5:30 in the afternoon of a February day. Darkness had settled down. The street light was on at Maple Street. School had been out for two hours, but Melie Kate and Ruth hadn't come home.

For the tenth time, I pulled the shade aside at the side door, and looked up the road toward Maple Street. Still no sign of them; only a solitary man with an empty lunch pail, striding home after work.

I turned the fire out under the supper, and went to the closet under the stairs for my coat and gloves. Clendenin was only seven blocks away. Somewhere along the road there must be news of Melie Kate and Ruth. None of their friends with telephones had seen them.

The front door closed behind me, and I was almost at the edge of the yard when I saw them coming down the road. They walked hand in hand, book satchels swinging, the street light making tall gaunt shadows on the road ahead of them.

I turned quickly and went indoors again before they could see me. I hung my coat in the closet and waited before the fire, my hands icy cold.

In a moment their footsteps sounded on the front porch. One of them whispered to the other. Then Melie Kate opened the front door.

"Hello," I said, casually.

"Hello."

Their faces were cold and wind-whipped, their eyes vaguely distant.

"Did something happen?" I asked.

"Nope," Melie Kate answered.

"Were you kept in?"

"No."

They put their book satchels on the table, and sat on the floor to undo their galoshes.

"I worried about you," I said. "Weren't you able to telephone me?"

"You're not our mother," Melie Kate said easily. "We can stay out without telling you, if we want to."

Anger surged to my throat. I clenched my hands, but the afternoon of fear and worry had been too much.

"Well, isn't this pretty!" I bit out angrily. "For two hours I've worried

myself sick, and the only thing wrong was that you were deliberately dis-
obeying me. You can both of you get this straight right now—until
Mother comes back, I *am* your mother here. You're to do exactly as I say.
Now trot yourselves out to the peach tree and get your own switches!"

Ruth looked up at me. Melie Kate began calmly to fasten her galoshes
again.

"Go on, Ruth," I snapped. "You, too. I'll be waiting in the
kitchen."

I turned and stalked from the room. My hands were trembling. Anger
was all through me, but as I walked, another feeling walked with me.
Fright. Somewhere a cord of security had frayed and loosened, and I stood
with the slack in my hands. Oh, Mother, I asked you what to do! You
didn't tell me!

I lit the fire under the supper, and stood waiting by the stove until they
came in. Then I took Ruth's switch and gave her five sharp licks on her
legs.

"Oh, Sister, please!" she wept. "I won't do it again. I didn't mean to,
Sister."

"You can go to your room now," I said.

She ran, weeping, from the kitchen. I turned to Melie Kate. She stood
before me, her face as calm and inscrutable as ever. My arms were leaden.
This wasn't right. I knew it wasn't right, but I had tried to find another
way. This had been coming on for a long, long time. "Turn around," I
said.

When it was finished, she turned and looked at me again, her face
white, her eyes narrow wells of fury. "I don't believe I care for any
supper," she said steadily. "I'm not very hungry tonight."

"Supper's ready in half an hour," I answered.

She went from the kitchen, through the dining-room, across the
living-room. Steadily and even, her footsteps went on up the stairs to her
room. Her bedroom door closed carefully.

I stood there a long moment in the silence. Then I laid the switch on
the table and went over to the stove. I took the lid off the pot of potatoes:
they bubbled noisily in the water. The meat loaf was sizzling in the oven,
the tomatoes were waiting in the icebox, the beans were almost done. The
egg custard was in four bowls, waiting on the table. There was nothing
anywhere to tell me what to do.

When supper was ready, I went to the landing and called Melie Kate
and Ruth. No answer. I went upstairs to their room and knocked on the

door. No sound from within. I turned into my room and found Ruth there, rummaging in my laundry bag.

"What are you looking for, Ruth?"

Her voice was high and tearful. "I can't find a handkerchief."

I opened my top dresser drawer and handed her one of mine. "Here you are. Now come on down to supper."

She followed me downstairs, into the kitchen. "I can help," she said, still in that meek, high voice.

"All right. Take the tomatoes in."

She picked up the bowl from the table and stood waiting. "We didn't do anything wrong," she said. "We played at Evelyn's."

"You've always asked me before."

"I'll remember next time."

"Well, that makes me feel much better." I turned and grinned at her. "You can have two helpings of egg custard for that promise."

She grinned back. Then she drew a big breath. "You shouldn't have whipped Melie Kate, though, Sister. She won't forgive you like I did. She might even run off." She nodded her head wisely. "She won't say she's sorry, Sister."

Melie Kate still hadn't come down by 8:00 o'clock. It was past Ruth's bedtime. Her lessons were finished, and there was nothing else to talk about without her unspoken words looking out at me again. I gave her her bath and put her to bed in my room. Then I went downstairs and fixed a tray for Melie Kate. I tiptoed upstairs and knocked on her door. Still no sound inside. I turned the knob. The door was unlocked. I opened it and stood on the threshold of the room.

It was dark except for the light from the flame in the gas stove. Melie Kate sat crosslegged in front of the stove, drawing on a piece of paper, her crayons and paper scattered all around her.

"Here's your supper," I said. I stepped inside and set the tray on a chair. "You'd better eat or you won't feel well tomorrow."

"I'm not hungry," she answered without looking up.

"There's meat loaf with gravy."

She didn't answer. The crayons went on making smooth markings on the paper. The light from the flame made shining lights in Melie Kate's hair.

She said, "Why don't you turn the light on?"

Her voice was as cool and independent as ever. Something like anger prickled over me again. Not only anger: she made me feel cornered, inexperienced.

I closed the door and reached over to snap the light switch on at the wall. As the room ceased to be shadows and dark, the wall across from me leaped forth in brilliant, garish color. The whole side of the plaster wall had been drawn on with crayon—people, houses, landscapes, strange lines with no meaning. Red, black, green, yellow—every color of the crayon box.

Suddenly a very strange and beautiful thing happened. "Oh, Melie Kate—" My eyes had tears. I couldn't help it. "It's beautiful, Melie! I didn't know you could draw like that."

Her head turned up toward me.

"It *is* beautiful, Melie Kate. It's everything there is, isn't it? It's my music, and Father's medicine, and Mother's pupils—" She wasn't understanding me, but what did it matter? I had only just understood. "Anyway, I didn't know you felt like that."

As suddenly, too, her sullenness was gone. She jumped to her feet and ran to the wall. "Here's Mother," she said, eagerly. "I had to stand on a chair—I couldn't make her big enough. Here's our house, and out here is where Papa goes. And here's how I felt when I was mad." Her fingers traced the meaningless lines, and she turned and laughed up at me. I laughed, too, and she turned back to the wall. "This is Ruthie. She's hit her head. And look, Sister!" She turned again, her eyes shining. "This is a dress that I want some day. It's blue, and all softish and silky-ish."

I sat on the bed and rolled over until I looked at the ceiling. "I want a blue dress, too," I said. "But how can we get them now with a wall that has to be all painted over?"

"It washes," she said.

In a moment I answered, "Oh, what does it matter? This is our house. This is your room. We don't have to wash it off if we don't want to. Let's leave it there to look at when we want to."

Ah, yes, I must have it before me, to remind me at times. Where had I dared step into footsteps that hadn't belonged to me? I was still only "Sister." I hadn't known before that no one can step into another's footsteps. I hadn't been careful enough with this little girl who had to stand on a chair to draw her Mother big enough.

I clasped my hands beneath my head. "What are you going to do when you're grown, Melie Kate?"

She came over and sat on the bed by me. The vibration was quiet between us now. "I think I'll make up dresses for people," she said.

"Dresses?"

She nodded. "I could. I made up a goblin costume for Miss Patterson at school once. You remember."

"I remember. Last fall."

"I could make up patterns for Ruthie now, if you'd sew them for me."

I turned my head to look at her. "What's wrong with Ruth's clothes?"

"She has to wear my dresses, mostly, and they don't look right on her. I'm thin and she's—she's sort of roundish."

"Who told you that—your art teacher?"

She shook her head. "No one told me. I know what looks right. I wish she had a yellow dress with pleats in it— Wait. I'll show you." She went to the closet and took down a big square box from the second shelf. I sat up, and when she came back we opened the box on the bed between us.

There were stacks of papers and drawings inside. There were paper dolls cut from catalogues and pasted on sheets of paper. There were pencil drawings, and patterns cut from newspapers.

Melie Kate handed me a drawing made on a small piece of brown wrapping paper. "Here's the one I mean, Sister."

It was an awkward, crude sketch, but I saw what she meant. The dress should be yellow, with pleats—

"Here's the blue one I want," Melie Kate was saying. "This is Mother's. This is yours, Sister—it's prettiest of all, isn't it?"

"Except that I'd never look right in a skirt as full as that."

"Yes, you would, too. You're thin."

We were still looking through the sheaves of papers, when I heard Little Doc's step on the gravel road outside. I looked up from my lapful of drawings.

"For heaven's sake!" I exclaimed. "It's almost nine o'clock, Melie Kate, and your supper is cold as ice again."

We looked at each other and laughed.

"Well, you can't get out of eating it," I said. "I'll warm it up just one more time. Come on down and Little Doc and I will have a snack with you."

I ran downstairs to unbolt the side door for Little Doc. I knew that Melie Kate would follow with the tray.

I knew, too, what I had to say to Little Doc when she was in bed. Melie Kate was almost ten years old—she wasn't a baby any longer. We had a new partner in the house. And somewhere, soon, we would have to find the money for a yellow dress with pleats, and a blue dress that was all softish and silky-ish.

# XVIII

THEN IT WAS the first Sunday in May, and Mother was coming home!

The air was heavy with magnolia scent that day; the earth was sweet and cool. Melie Kate and Ruth had spent all day, Saturday, raking the yard and straightening the stones around Mother's precious flower beds. All the jonquils were straight yellow sentinels.

Indoors, the house shone like a pin. I had scrubbed and scoured for a week. There wasn't a spot of dust left; not a feather under the beds. The pans gleamed in the kitchen. The curtains were newly starched and hung. Supper was ready to be put on the stove as soon as the car turned in at the driveway.

At four o'clock in the afternoon, I saw that Melie Kate and Ruth were bathed and dressed, their hair brushed until it stood on end with electricity. Then I sent them downstairs to sit on the swing and watch for the car to turn down from Main Street. It should be arriving any moment now— Mother and Little Doc had left Booneville early in the morning.

After I was dressed, I went through all the upstairs rooms again, straightening the covers on the beds, placing the rugs at their perfect angle. On the table by Mother's bed was a bowl of blue starflowers that Melie Kate had picked in the woods, and another bowl full of wiggling doodlebugs that Ruth had conjured up from their holes in the sandy dust of the driveway. Everything was ready for Mother to come back to.

I stood in the doorway of the bedroom, feeling a small core of fear in me again. What would happen when Mother saw the empty chair by the fireplace, the house that had no clumping step on the stairs, no car to turn down from Main Street on the stroke of six? All my scrubbing and scouring had only served to make the emptiness more naked in the house.

There were footsteps running across the porch. Then a crash and silence.

I turned from the doorway and ran down the stairs.

"What happened, Melie Kate?"

She still sat swinging. Ruth was nowhere to be seen, and at one end of the porch, where the clematis vine had been was an empty gap.

"Ruth fell off the porch," Melie Kate said.

"Oh, for heaven's sakes!"

I went to the end of the porch, and looked down on her, tangled and dirty in the mass of clematis vines. She grinned up at me. "I'm not hurt."

"Maybe not, but you're dirty as a pig. What on earth were you doing?"

"Chasing a butterfly, but I missed him."

Melie Kate bounded out of the swing and ran to the edge of the steps. "There they are, Sister! There's Mother!"

I looked up the road. The car had already reached the corner of Maple Street. I could see Mother in the front seat with Little Doc.

"Get up quickly and brush yourself off, Ruth. Run out to the corner with Melie and maybe Little Doc will let you ride the running-board in." I laughed as I turned to wait for the car at the driveway. "Mother wouldn't know you without a couple of broken arms, anyway, I suppose."

Mother had supper in bed that night. Little Doc hadn't let us talk to her more than fifteen minutes.

"Dr. Shipton says she's strong as a horse," he said, "but we're not taking any chances. She's going right to her room and rest."

Mother turned and looked at him. "You'll be the hardest doctor in town, Little Doc. I haven't seen my two youngest in over six months."

"Well, you'll be seeing them for fifty more 'six months,' " I said. "Little Doc's right. We can talk tomorrow."

Mother's mouth was firm, but her eyes danced. "I can see right now that I've two children to teach who's boss around here again. I'll go to bed now, Little Doc, but after supper, I'm to talk with Melie Kate and Ruth for thirty minutes."

"Thirty minutes," I promised. "I'll send them up at 7:30."

Little Doc picked up Mother's bag, and she followed him upstairs.

"Come on, Melie and Ruth," I said. "You can fix Mother's tray if you'll be careful."

So far, so good. Little Doc had been wise. Mother had been whisked upstairs before she could feel anything in the house but our love and excitement at having her home again. Maybe by tomorrow everything would be easier.

When I was ready for bed that night, there was still a crack of light in the hall, from under Mother's door.

I knocked. "You should be in bed, Mother."

"I don't go to bed with the chickens yet," she answered. "Come in for a moment."

I opened the door carefully. "Little Doc won't like it!"

Her eyes twinkled. "Well, close the door and he won't hear you."

She sat in her rocker, her woolly robe thrown over her shoulders. I closed the door behind me and leaned against it. "I'm an old busybody, Mother, and you won't like it, but you should be lying down after such a long trip home."

She moved her head with the old, impatient gesture. Her voice was edged. "I've thirty more years to sleep in that bed by myself. I'm in no hurry the first night."

Swiftly I went over to her. "Oh, Mother, we didn't think! We didn't think!" Why hadn't we taken the old blue bed out and put the smaller bed in its place? Why hadn't we thought to shift the furniture?

She moved impatiently again. Then her face changed. She held me at arms' length and frowned. "You're so thin, Sister!"

Relief was so great in me that it swelled to my throat. "Now don't start that again, Mother. I've always been thin."

"And my musician's hands," she said, looking down at my hands in hers. "What a hard, strange road they've been on."

"I didn't use enough cold cream, that's all that's the matter with them." I tried to pull my hands away from her sight, but her grip tightened and she pulled me down to her lap. I sat there awkwardly, ill at ease. Mother's voice was soft when she spoke to me.

"Don't you know that I know everything that you're thinking, Sister?" she said. "Don't you know that your eyes look out at me from every corner and say, 'He's gone, Mother, but we're still here'?"

I couldn't look at her. My throat hurt. "I was afraid for you to come home."

"I know. Every scrubbed board in my house shouts it."

"I didn't know what else to do."

One arm reached around me and held me close against her, the other cradled my head on her shoulder. "When I came in the front door this afternoon, he stood big and proud waiting for me, Sister. He was in Little Doc's eyes—his crooked cowlick—trying so hard to be the man of the house—" Mother's voice always halted when she was trying to tell me something. "He was in Melie Kate's little blue and yellow dresses—Ruthie's happy grin. He was in every corner of my house. Every corner—" In a moment she added "—my house with the four strong pillars."

The silence in the room grew huge and still. Mother rocked the chair. Her cheek was on my forehead. "But every night I thought of one little girl of mine who had no one to tuck her in."

I couldn't answer. I was too tired, and the pain in my throat was too thick. In this moment I was a little girl again—a tired little girl, whose job was done, and who wanted to be rocked to sleep while her head rested in the warmth of her mother's shoulder.

# XIX

WE CUT DOWN the old sweet-gum tree by the front porch steps on my eighteenth birthday.

Bill was there. He had three days' leave from Dr. Ledbetter's office. It was Little Doc's day off from Frank's, and we were all sitting on the front porch, shelling peanuts. Bill rose from the swing suddenly, walked to the steps and peered up through the branches of the tree.

"This tree is dead," he said to Mother. "Why don't you get it cut down?"

Mother didn't look up from her sewing. "I've kept putting it off. It's been the stone in front of Lazarus' tomb since we moved here."

"Then it's time it was cut!"

Little Doc jumped up from where he was sitting, leaning against one of the porch pillars. "We could do it, Bill! We've got a cross-cut saw and an ax in the basement. It's been a long time since we've cut a tree down." He crossed to the screen door and opened it. "All right, Mother?"

"It's all right if you want to do the work," she said.

"Well, it's not all right with me," I said. "I don't want it down. The only thing wrong with it is that tent caterpillars have killed some of the top limbs."

"Oh, go take a look, Sister," Little Doc said. "The whole top is dead."

"A man from the nursery hasn't said so!"

Mother spoke quietly. "It's been in front of the steps long enough, anyway. Sooner or later someone is going to trip over those big roots, and then it will be too late to argue about it. I'm surprised that it hasn't happened long ago." She turned toward the door. "Close the screen, Little Doc. You're letting flies in."

Bill stuffed a handful of peanuts in his pocket, and he and Little Doc were on their way through the house to the basement door. In a moment I heard their voices from underneath the porch.

"It isn't fair, Mother," I said. "You haven't given it a chance."

"I've been watching it since I came back, Mary. When a thing is finished, get rid of it. There'll be a lot more things disappear from around this house before the year's out, I'm reckoning."

I got up stiffly from the swing, and went indoors and up to my room. I lay across my bed and looked out through the window and the great spreading branches. The sweet-gum tree was my tree: it had been outside my window for the twelve years that I had been in this room. What had Mother called it? The stone in front of Lazarus' tomb? It was a shield for me: the screen through which I looked out on the world from my bedroom window.

Bill and Little Doc's footsteps came back up the basement stairs, and through the house to the porch. They had the saw and ax with them—I could hear as Mother scraped her chair farther over on the porch to make room for them to come through the door. I pulled the shade down at the window, and lay listening for the shudder that would go through the huge tree at the first stroke of the ax.

In a few moments I left my room and went downstairs again. I was behaving childishly: the tree was dead—

There were lemons and cookies in the pantry. I fixed lemonade and took a tray to the porch. Melie Kate and Ruth sat on the swing, excitement wriggling all over them as they watched the saw bite deeper into the wood. There was the clean dry smell of sawdust. Bill's shirt was already sticking to his back. Little Doc's face glistened brownly in the sun.

"Here's ambrosia for your second wind," I said. "It's spiked with ginger ale, so be careful."

Bill stood back and wiped his face with the back of his hand. "Peanut butter cookies?" he asked.

"No. Oatmeal cookies. You need sustenance."

Mother's voice was gleefully caustic. "He needs a good roast beef sandwich more than anything else. He's going to discover in a minute that sawing a tree down isn't the same exercise as jabbing somebody with a hypodermic needle. I'm waiting to see him capsize."

Bill took one of the glasses from the tray and handed it to her. "From the fly to the spider," he said with his grin. "From the guillotined to the knitting woman."

Mother laid her sewing down and took the glass. I set the tray on the table so I could pour the lemonade.

"Somebody's coming," Little Doc said.

A car turned at our corner, drove up to the side of the yard and stopped. I stood with the pitcher in my hand, as the man opened the car door, swung his long legs onto the ground and came toward the porch. Little Doc went to meet him.

"Do you know who it is?" Mother asked.

"It's John MacCreighton," I answered slowly. "It's Mr. MacCreighton. He's a minister."

Bill straightened the pitcher in my hands, and laughed. "Keep your eyes on the boat, Spareribs. We're shipping lemonade." I blushed to the roots of my hair. Again I had done something foolish when the minister from Granite Hill was around. This time lemonade had almost gone down Mother's neck.

There were two crates of strawberries in the back of Mr. MacCreighton's new car. He had brought them in from Cull Brant's. He and Bill and Little Doc hauled the two big boxes into the house, and then he stood by one of the porch pillars and searched for something in his pockets. "Lizzie Brant sent her recipe for preserves," he said, frowning. "Half wild strawberries and half cultivated ones, she said." The paper wasn't in his pants pockets, his coat pockets, even his shirt pocket. "She put it somewhere so I wouldn't forget it," he insisted. "Guess I must have left it in the car."

He was off the porch and striding toward the car, but I was running after him. "Wait a minute," I said. "I've found it!"

He stood still and I unpinned it from the tail of his coat.

"Mother always had to pin Father's notes on the pages of Shakespeare," I laughed, handing the paper back to him.

We went back to the porch, and he stood leaning against the pillar again. I sat on the steps by Little Doc.

"I've just thought what we can do for supper," Mother said. "We'll have a picnic." Her eyes were dancing and her mouth had the quirk to it.

Melie Kate and Ruth almost fell out of the swing.

"We've got lots of wood," Ruth said. "We can burn up the tree."

"That's not anything to eat for supper," Little Doc said.

"It's five o'clock now," Mother went on. "By the time we have everything ready, it will be six." She rolled her sewing up and turned to Mr. MacCreighton. "You're to stay. It's too late to head back country for supper." Before he could open his mouth, she had risen and was at the front door. "Melie Kate and Ruth can collect some dry sticks in the woods—I'll make biscuits for shortcake while the men get the fire started."

Melie Kate left the swing. "I'll make sandwiches, Mother."

"We'll need hot dogs and buns and pickles," I said.

"And ants," Bill put in dryly.

"And my girl," Little Doc added.

We all stared at him. "What girl, Little Doc?"

He was casual. "Oh—a girl about so high." His hand measured a height that would come to his chin. "Sort of a blonde."

"For heaven's sake!"

"Her name is Alice Anita Awalt," Melie Kate announced. "He had a date with her last Friday night. I think they went to a picture show."

"Well!" I said.

Mother said, "All right, Little Doc. See if she can come if you want to and you can stop at the grocery store on your way after her."

"Oh, she'll come," he said loftily. "We had a date for later this evening, anyway."

Bill whistled, Mr. MacCreighton looked at Little Doc speculatively, and I had a strange feeling of sitting by myself on the step. I had never thought of Little Doc with a girl. We had always had such fun together when we went places with each other.

Mr. MacCreighton stepped back suddenly from the pillar where he had been leaning, and struck one hand quickly against the other. Two yellow and black insects buzzed angrily away from the porch.

"Yellow-jackets!" I cried. "There's another one on your coat collar."

Bill reached forward and brushed it off with a stroke that killed it. Mr. MacCreighton laughed and blew on his hand.

"They stung you!" I said. I reached for his hand and turned it palm up: there were two red welts there. "I think soda will do it."

"Mud is better," Little Doc said.

Mr. MacCreighton said nothing. In a moment Bill said, "Fine thing! A doctor on the porch—the only doctor on the porch—and no one cares a hoot about asking his advice." I looked up to laugh at his wry voice, but the look on his face stopped me. It was then that I realized that I still held Mr. MacCreighton's hand, and neither of us had moved for a long second.

There was a crescent moon that night. A crescent moon and a silver star in a black velvet sky. Long after the picnic was over, and Mother and Melie Kate and Ruth had gone indoors, Bill and I sat leaning against the trunk of the fallen sweet-gum tree, watching the dying embers of the fire. John MacCreighton had left for the back country right after dark. Little Doc and Alice Anita had gone for their movie an hour before.

I said, "Little Doc told me about your plans for his school next year, Bill. I think it's perfectly wonderful."

Bill rumpled his hair embarrassedly. "Your brother works fast these days. I didn't even discuss it with him until we were building the fire tonight."

"I still think it's wonderful. I don't believe you even know how much it means to him. He never talks about things that he really cares about."

"It's no more than Big Doc did for me. Ledbetter was interested too, when I discussed Little Doc with him, so I thought we might as well grab the chance while it was hot. If Little Doc works with us in the office all summer, he'll have almost all his tuition by fall. I'll see that he makes it all right."

"Six years of it?—"

Bill's hand was rumpling his hair again. "Four times during my six years, I would have given up if someone hadn't been back of me. Anyway," he added lightly, "it looks as if I'm having to put you back on the shelf. I might as well take something in exchange."

I settled closer against the tree and looked up at the sky and the moon. "Didn't you have a fraternity pin like that once, Bill?" I asked. "I remember a gold chain that held the star onto the moon."

"It was a club pin," he answered. "Mimi Abbott lost it down a well or something."

"Mimi Abbott lost it in the collection in her jewel box," I answered sarcastically. "You gave her your class ring, and your pin and your basketball medal."

He sighed, "Mimi was a great gal in high school days."

"Mimi swallowed more club pins and fraternity pins than any other girl in school. You were older than the others. You should have known better."

Bill asked, "Could you be jealous—by some remote chance?"

Again the undertone of seriousness was in his light answer. There wasn't anything else for me to say now. I knew what Bill had come home for this time—I couldn't put it off much longer.

"I was always jealous of Mimi," I said quietly. "She had curly hair."

Then we were both silent. Bill reached for a twig at his side and snapped it in pieces. Finally he said, "I never thought I'd be jealous of an Ichabod Crane with a preserve recipe pinned on his coat tails."

My heart leaped to my throat. I sat up straight. "Bill! Bill, you're being perfectly ridiculous!" This wasn't what I had thought he was going to say.

"Mr. MacCreighton is the minister at Granite Hill—he came in with two crates of strawberries—Cull Brant would have had to haul them all the way in his wagon if he hadn't—"

Bill sat up straight and tossed the twigs toward the coals. "You're not making a bit of sense," he said.

He turned to me, his arms were strong around my shoulders, and he kissed me, there with the gold-black glow of the embers before us and the night wind hushed around us.

His cheek was rough on mine and he laughed at me—the laugh that one saves for a child. "Oh, Mary, I love you so much that I can't imagine what the rest of time will be like without you around me all my life. I wonder what I'll ever do."

His hands were on my shoulders, and he held me off from him.

My voice was shaken. "I don't know, Bill. I—"

"I don't know, either."

He leaned back against the tree again and turned to look toward the coals. "I refuse to be Uncle Bill and dandle your children on my knee," he said wryly. "I'm not the type to send anonymous love notes with orchids on every birthday of yours, either."

"Oh, Bill—"

Suddenly it seemed that so many things were slipping away from me today. Little Doc and his girl—then Little Doc leaving for St. Louis as soon as school was out—even the sweet-gum tree that had always been by my window. If Bill were gone, what would I have left? There was no dream of a Conservatory to hold to any more: I had long ago decided that the best I could do would be to study from Professor Howell and perhaps try for a scholarship in a small school somewhere in a year or two. What did I want now?

But Mother had spoken some words to me that afternoon. "When a thing is finished, Mary, get rid of it." It was a strength to know what to let go of.

"Bill," I said. "Bill—" It took a deep breath for me to go on. "Everything's all mixed up for me right now. Sometimes I don't know what I want at all any more—but there's one thing that I know, and a year hasn't changed it a bit. Your road isn't my road, Bill."

His voice was even. "What is your road?"

I listened for an answer. I said, "I don't even know that, Bill." I laughed. "When I was a little girl, Father used to laugh at me because if something didn't turn up as I wanted it to, I would say, 'Maybe it isn't time for it yet.' Maybe it isn't time for me to know what I'm going to do yet. The only thing that I've always been sure of, is that I have to be ready for it when it comes. The road to St. Louis isn't it."

I couldn't tell whether Bill had understood me or not. He hadn't moved. I said, "Bill, once you had to make a decision for yourself, that you couldn't let anything stand in front of—not even your feeling for Father. This is almost the same kind of decision for me to make—" He still didn't move. "You've always been very dear to me—you know that—"

It was a long moment before he answered. In that moment, the last glow of the coals dimmed into the rest of the darkness. The evening was over.

Bill stood up and pulled me up after him. When he spoke, his voice was the one of the Bill that I had known from years before. "Don't ever let anyone keep you from going your own road, Spareribs. It's the only signpost anyone can trust."

Relief swept over me in a wave. "Oh, Bill— Thank you—"

"Don't thank me," he said, lightly. "That's what Big Doc said to me when I made my decision. I think he'd want it handed on to you at this point."

He started toward the house, then turned to speak again. "Careful when you hit the terrace here—there's loose limbs all over the place."

# XX

BIG JAKE GRANTHER stood at our side door. The dust of the back country was on his faded jeans, and his face was brown from the hot June sun.

"Good morning, Mr. Granther," I said. "It's been a long time since you've knocked on our side door."

"It's been a long spell since ye've been out our way, Miss Mary. Everybody well?"

"Everybody's well," I said. "Your house, too?"

He nodded. "All's well." He leaned one bony hand against the door casing and looked off toward the edge of the yard. "Wonder could I have words with Miz Doc?"

I hesitated. "She's giving a piano lesson—" Beyond him, parked by the side of the road, was his wagon loaded high with melons for the curb market. A half-hour might mean loss of the early morning customers. "I'll call her. Please come in."

"No, thank'ee," he said. "I'll wait here." He took his hand from the door and pulled his tobacco sack from the pocket of his jeans.

When Mother came from the living-room, I walked back to the kitchen and closed the door behind me. Something in Jake's manner had made me vaguely uneasy. It might have been his odd request to speak with Mother. Those weather-beaten faces at our side door had always meant, "I want Big Doc—tell him Ezzie's baby's a-bornin'." It was the town faces at the front door that asked, "Is your Mother in? I want to see about piano lessons." But then it might have been the unfamiliar look in Jake Granther's eyes when he spoke to me. A keen, straight look.

The kitchen door opened in a moment and Mother stood there. "Mary, do you have any plans for this summer?"

"What kind of plans?"

"Studying, or working."

I shook my head. "There's no money for lessons. I thought maybe there would be a job so I could start again in the fall."

"How would teaching appeal to you?"

Suddenly my heart was a trip hammer. "Piano teaching?" She nodded. "I suppose if you could start at fourteen with no conservatory work, I can start at eighteen without any."

"Yes." Her eyes were seeing something far beyond me. Perhaps that little pig-tailed girl of years ago, riding off down the road on the brown horse, Penny, a music roll tied to the saddle horn. "Yes. Well!" She spoke briskly. "Jake Granther says they've bought their new organ at Granite Hill, and they've come for you to show them how to play it. They're six who can study until school starts, he says." She hesitated. "It's twenty miles back country."

I know what she meant. Twenty miles back country with the rutted roads and uncertain trips to the curb markets, might mean a month before I could get home again. I said, "I'm eighteen, Mother. I'd like to go."

"You come discuss details with him," she said. "He wants to pick you up on his way back from the curb market this afternoon."

She closed the door and I heard her footsteps go back to the living-room. I sat where I was for a long moment before I went to the side door to see Jake Granther. My mind flashed back to a memory of a year before. Jake had sat next to me on Phineas Granther's front porch; he had rolled a cigarette from the papers in his pocket as he told me about the organ that would be waiting for me in the Granite Hill church in a year or two. I remembered what I had thought then: my teaching was never to be in the back country—my teaching wasn't to begin for years and years. The Conservatory was to be first.

Yet—here was the moment that I had also known would come, since the first time I had sat on the fourth step behind the banisters to hear Mother give a piano lesson. The voice at the door had come for me! I had thought it would be the front door, though! No matter. It had come. It had come early, but it had come. And what a teacher I would be! My pupils would do what Mother's did, and I would teach as Mother did. I would have my own lesson book and sit on the porch after supper to mark down the day's lessons. I would probably even ride a horse as Mother had done. I could see myself waving from the road as we went by, and the people in the houses waving back. "There goes Big Doc's gal," they would say. "Growed-up, now. I hear she's most as good as her Ma a-teachin'." A shiver went down my spine.

I rose from the chair and went into the dining-room, toward the side door.

"Mary," Mother called from the living-room. She opened the door and spoke to me again. "You'd better use my big suitcase. It's under the quilts in my closet." Her eyes were soft and her mouth had the quirk to it. "I wish I had time to help you pack, but I teach until after two this afternoon. Don't forget your music lists."

The sun was two hours past our chimney when Jake Granther returned for me. He swung Mother's big suitcase in the back of the empty wagon, and gave me a hand up to the high seat beside him.

The family stood in a row to see me off. Melie Kate and Ruth were wide-eyed with awe at my close proximity to the big man with the black beard. Little Doc, home on his lunch hour from Frank's, was stolidly expressionless at our parting. In two days he was leaving for St. Louis. It would be a long time before we were together again. Slyly he handed me an old beanshooter that he had made when he was in Clendenin. It was the one with the three nicks in the handle for the three boys who had tried to take it away from him.

"It's for luck," he said.

Mother put a small gray ledger in my lap. My lesson book! A lesson book and a beanshooter! "I know how David felt," I said, and I laughed with excitement. The rocky dirt road to the back country was the road to a Glorious Adventure now.

But look! Coming down that road was a small figure with a music satchel in its hand. Mother's two o'clock pupil. Goliath! Suddenly the adventure dropped away and hard panic was there from underneath. "Mother." I gripped her hand. "Mother, I've never taught before. How will I know?"

Mother's other hand pulled my head down to hers. "Don't you worry, Sister. You'll know." Her voice was easy, but her eyes looked as my heart felt. "You'll know," she said again.

Jake Granther flipped the reins and clucked to the horses, and we were bumping down the rutted road. I clutched the lesson book and Little Doc's beanshooter, and looked straight between old Samson's ears. The road ahead was a strange rocky road that I had never seen before. Heat rays made shimmering will-o'-the-wisps.

In my chest was a shriveled lump where a moment before had been a full-blown balloon of excitement. Suppose I couldn't teach after all? Suppose I couldn't even begin a lesson? Oh, surely I should know that. That fourth step behind the banisters had a worn spot on the varnish from the years that I had sat there, listening to all the lessons that Mother had begun and ended. Only now all those lessons seemed to have rolled into one big lesson—no beginning, no ending. Only pieces from one whole.

After a long time I turned and asked of Jake Granther's profile. "Am I to live at your house?"

"Yore Ma said to. My house is easy walkin' to the church house, and that's where ye'll be teachin'."

His elbows leaned on sharp bony knees, and suddenly I had a picture of rows of grizzled Ichabod Cranes, at rows of organs, long grasshopper legs doubled up until their knees bumped the bottom of the keyboard with every pump of the pedal.

I said, "Are there to be any boys to teach?"

Jake thought for a moment. "Tom Johnson said his young'un aims to take. He's got a hawg of his own to pay with." He turned then, and his eyes twinkled. "I got a girl yore age."

I knew what to say. "I'll teach her then for my board."

"We was aimin' fer her to take," he answered. "We got pertaters and peanuts extry."

"Well, Father said you have another girl. I'll teach her for them."

We must have gone a quarter of a mile before he answered that. "Her name's Dorcas. Her Ma died when she was borned and she ain't right in the haid. She sings funny-like." He jerked impatiently on the reins and squinted at the blinding sun. "If them horses git a-movin' we'll git thar 'bout sundown."

The road wound on, and the sun dipped lower. Jake had said right. The wagon topped the rise of Granite Hill as the last red and gold ribbons streaked behind the hickory grove. A great field of cotton stretched on either side of the road, and upon the side of the next hill was a small white house.

Jake pointed a gnarled finger at the fields of curved green rows. "Thet's my ground," he said. "My Pa give it to me when I was eleven y'ar old."

The clean brown smell of fresh earth was in the air.

"It smells good," I said.

He looked over the new-turned furrows, and pulled out his snuffbox. "Hit was a day like this'n the first time I ever plowed thet ground. Pa's homestead was over thet hill yonder afore he went to Mount Horeb. He hitched up the team and said, 'This field's yorn, Jake, soon's ye larn to plow it.' "

He stopped, and I felt that he wanted me to say something. "You must have been proud, Mr. Granther."

He chuckled. "I was skeered. Skeered plumb holler, I kin tell ye." He chuckled again. "Pa'd planted corn that spring, and them little green shoots was no taller'n my elbow. They kept a-whisperin' as plain like. 'Don't git thet iron tooth too clost my roots,' they said. 'Don't you let it git too clost.' "

His face became grave, and his hand still held the unopened snuffbox. "Sometimes I wisht I could remember the feelin' I got thet mornin' when Pa walked down thet road and left me thar all by myself. Everybody ought to remember the feelin' they git the first time they start workin' their own ground." He shook his head. "I git thinkin' most back thar sometimes, and then, Piff! Hit goes through. Like leanin' on a fence post and it ain't thar. Then I git to thinkin' maybe thar warn't no beginnin'. Maybe I was born in plowin'."

I wanted to say something, but then I saw the other white building that I hadn't seen before.

"That looks like a church," I said.

Jake nodded. "Reckon thar'll be quite a meetin' thar tonight, too. Folks thought you might play the orgin fer 'em."

Something inside me turned sickeningly. Oh, not so soon! Let me wait until tomorrow. Let me wait right here until tomorrow! But the wagon rumbled on, past the church, past the field, and up the road to the house on the hill.

We walked down the hill after supper. Gert, who was my age, and Dorkie, the queer one, were with us this time. It was dark, with white scaly clouds in a still sky.

"Mackeral sky," Jake said. "Rain tomorror."

We walked down the road, past the field, and up the path to the whitewashed, one-room church house. A wagon was drawn up by the well.

"Hit's them Bascoms," Gert said disdainfully. "They're allus fust come."

The Bascoms sat in a long row on the second bench from the front. They had lit the four wall lamps, and a dim yellow light filled the square church room. Heavy green curtains had been pulled in front of the pulpit to make the room into a meetinghouse.

Jake strode up the aisle. "Miz Bascom, meet Big Doc's gal." Mrs. Bascom smiled carefully, and Mr. Bascom leaned over the bench to shake my hand in a horny grip. "Pleased to meetcha, Teacher." The four little Bascoms stared as one great solemn eye.

Granny Bascom leaned her hands on her cane and said doubtfully,

"She hain't so big."

"Thet's cause she don't eat nothin'," Gert explained loudly. "Shoulda' seen her at supper. Two biscuits and a spoonin' of grease beans. She won't git no man thet'a way." They all laughed, and Gert smiled archly in her wisdom.

I went up to the organ. It stood shiny and new against the thick green curtains, the lid thrown back waiting for me. I sat on the bench and pressed my fingers down on the cold white keys. There was no sound. The four little Bascoms giggled in whispers. "Teacher fergot to pump it." My feet fumbled for the long flat pedals, and I pumped them with all my might. A great roaring chord swelled out and echoed back in overtones from the walls. Another chord, softer this time, to swallow the shakiness in my hands, and then a melody. Any melody. Anything to start thinking in.

In a moment I felt safer; wrapped around in the music from the "looking over" that had already begun. I played carefully; nothing too far away from these people, nothing condescending. Mendelssohn's "Spring Song"; "The Lost Chord." The plantation songs, a hymn or so.

I turned around. "What's your favorite, Granny Bascom?"

Her rheumy eyes were misty. " 'The Old Rugged Cross,' thank'ee kindly." She hummed it in a quaver as I played it.

"And yours, Mrs. Bascom?"

" 'The Jericho Road,' maybe."

"I don't know that one. Is there music?"

Jeptha, Tom Johnson's young 'un, had come in. He propped a hymn book on the scrolled rack in front of me, and held a lamp by my left shoulder to light the pages of notes. I heard Granny Bascom humming again.

"Sing, Jeptha, you and Gert. Let's all sing." Jeptha and Gert started with me, and the four little Bascoms burst out in the middle of the second line.

It was when we reached the last verse that I became conscious of other voices than the Granthers and the Bascoms in the singing back of me. I heard a horse neigh in the woods; a wagon creak up to the well. We finished the hymn, and a strange voice called out, "Sweet Hour of Prayer." I was glad that I knew that one without music.

Under the voices was the sound of more wagons in the yard, and coughing motors of rattling trucks. Footsteps clumped up the three plank steps and down the bare boards of the aisle. Long, heavy boot strides, and short lighter steps. Jeptha turned the pages for another hymn and whispers came from the front row.

"How you payin' Teacher?"

"Preserves. I done canned thirty-six quarts. How're you?"

"I got money."

Incredulous whispers swooped down like bees.

"Where'd you git it?"

"I chopped cotton," defiantly. "Pa said I could spend it fer anything. Look! I got blood blisters."

I played quickly; quickly to drown something that seemed to cry out. My fingers wouldn't stop now. The music rolled on; the rhythm grew broader as more voices came in with more footsteps. Jake Granther sang mightily, his heavy boots beating time on the bare planked floor. Dorkie, the queer one, stood against the side of the bench at first, her strange high voice weaving a silver thread in the heavy-woven voices from the benches. Soon her head leaned full against my shoulders, but it was vaguely comfortable to play that way.

The words of the song, "And Isaiah said, 'Ho, all ye that thirsteth, Come ye to the waters—' " These people sang for music as they sang for rain. Jake Granther had said that six had planned to take lessons, but the room was full of children's voices. What would they get? I would ask the minister if I could have a meeting every Tuesday night. A singing meeting. I would take no pay for that. They could call it a Singing Practice, if they wanted to, and sing all their hymns and folk songs. I could teach them songs that I knew. Perhaps the one that Father loved to sing on cold winter evenings. "Jaybird sitting on a crooked limb, I cocked my gun and I shot at him, Said he, 'Young man, don't you do thet agin ,' Yip Yi, Yip Ti yi, Eat pa'ched corn and sit by the fire." Yes, they would like that one.

"Play two-hundred-six, Teacher. We got a quartet fer it." The four little Bascoms stood by the side of the organ and opened their mouths like sparrows. "Just like a tree-ee, that's planted by the wa-ters—" they sang.

Dorcas sat on the bench by my right arm now. Her queer-shaped hands were on the keys an octave above mine, and her fingers followed the pattern that mine were making.

"Can you play, Dorkie?"

"She picks 'em out," Jeptha answered by my ear. "I heered her after preachin' last Sunday."

"Will you play this, Dorkie, and let me rest a while?" She didn't look up. I slid down the bench, and she put her hands where mine had been. Not a break in the rhythm. The four voices sang on. Nothing had changed.

A strange, prickling feeling crept over me. Somewhere, sometime, this had all happened before. The room, the music, the twisted hands—it was happening ahead of me. Part of my dream, perhaps.

In a blinding flash I saw it again. It wasn't the dream. I was looking down on it; looking down from between banister posts. It was Mother at the piano, playing on and on, and behind a chair was a cowering little boy with vacant eyes. The room fills with music, and the little boy creeps closer until he stands at Mother's elbow. Suddenly his hands crash down on the keys. "Can you play, Rickie?" That furious pounding.

"This is horses!" he shrieks. "Someone hurt them."

Mother reaches down and holds his hands tightly in hers. "It's over now." That deafening silence and the stillness of the small figure. "It's over, Rickie."

"My name's Dorkie."

I looked down. I was standing by the bench, and my hands gripped Dorkie's until the knuckles were white. The room was still. The singing had stopped, and that voice in the silence was mine.

I knew what came next. I turned. "I want to teach you a song that I know. A song that Big Doc used to sing." The rows of faces smiled; brown, weather-beaten faces, small eager faces, old, wrinkled faces. "I want the men on this side of the aisle and the women on the other."

There was a scrambling for seats. The four little Bascoms tumbled over each other and shrilled excitedly. Granny Bascom picked up her cane and hobbled across the aisle.

Jake Granther stood in the doorway. His hands were in his pockets and his eyes watched the crowding people. I wanted him to look at me. I wanted to cry out, "Look, Jake Granther! Look what's happened! I'm teaching! I've always known how to teach. Remember what you said to me this afternoon? You said, 'Everybody ought to remember the feeling they get the first time they start plowing their own ground.' I want to remember this feeling all my life. It began just a moment ago. It began with Dorkie's head on my shoulders. No! No, it was Dorkie's hands on the keys of the organ." Strange, twisted hands—Rickie's hard pounding from a hurt heart—eyes behind the banisters, and another little girl riding down the road on a horse named Penny—it twists far, far back—I can't touch it any longer. "It's too far back, Jake, and I'm too tired to find it now. Later I'll think back—"

Dorkie's eyes were big and black in front of me. I put my hands on the keys again. "Listen, Dorkie. Listen closely. Watch my hands and pick this out. 'Jaybirds sitting on a crooked limb, I cocked my gun and I shot at him—'"

# XXI

I LAY AWAKE that night until long after the moon had sailed past the porch pillars. When we came back up the hill from the church, Gert and Dorcas had pulled three feather mattresses onto the porch, and Jake had taken his lamp and climbed the stairs to his room under the eaves.

The moon was silver and distant; the stars were scattered thinly in the open space of sky. I lay awake between the rough cool sheets, my mind as clear and peaceful as the feeling around me. Dorcas and Gert were asleep on their mattresses. For a while there had been a square of golden light in the yard from the window in Jake's room, and a mumbling drone that was the Bible lesson being read for church the next morning—but now the square was blotted out, the voice was still. I was alone in the sounds of the fields and the woods.

Something was waiting for me out there tonight. It was in the wide space around me, the soft wind that blew across the porch and brushed my face with light cool fingers. It was in the smell of dank swamp weed, the two mournful tones of the bullfrog, the call of the whippoorwill in the black woods. "Chip butter, white oak. Chip butter, white oak." Dorkie turned in her sleep and her hand reached across the floor boards until it touched my pillow. Something was very close to me, but my mind was too calmed to search for it now. "Chip butter, white oak. Chip butter . . . white oak . . . "

A clink of buckets and whispering voices wakened me the next morning. For a moment I stayed in space, trying to place the strange sensation of waking in the dark. The stars were spent glints in the sky. The moon was gone. Then the bullfrog croaked, and I was awake.

I dressed quickly and went through to the kitchen. A fire crackled in the black iron range. The breakfast biscuits were round white mounds in the pans on the table. Gert and Dorcas stood by the back door, lard buckets on their arms, the glow of the fire casting them in strange gold shadows.

"I'd like to go with you if you're milking," I said.

"You don't have to git up yit," Gert answered. "Flies don't bite fer an hour yit."

"I want to go," I said. "Wait until I get a sweater."

Then the back door closed behind us, and the three of us were picking our footsteps carefully down the hill toward the soft moos in the black shadow of the barn beyond. The morning mists were ghostly and damp. Dorkie stood stock still at the barn yard gate and said, "Listen, Teacher!" Far off was the faint moan of a hound. "Someone's daid!" she said hoarsely.

Gert unlatched the gate impatiently. "Don't pay no 'tention to her, Miss Mary. She's tetched."

She walked on across the barn yard, the milk buckets swinging with her stride, her hips settling solidly with each step. Gert was the strength and warmth of the sun at noon; Dorcas belonged with the mists and sounds of the gray morning.

At the barn, Gert and Dorcas pulled their stools into two stalls and slapped the cows on the rump. "Git over, Lady!" Gert said sharply. "Git on over, you gol-darned heifer!"

"I don't know how to milk," I said. "What else could I do?"

"You could git aigs. They's a couple nests up in the loft."

"Do I climb that ladder?"

"It ain't bad if ye're keerful." The sound of milk in the pails was a frothy, mushy sound now. "Better git the can on the bench out thar to put 'em in."

I climbed carefully up to the cool, fragrant hay. Two hens that had been roosting somewhere in the rafters close over my head, screamed and cackled as I crawled over to the nests by the window. They flew to the floor below in a flurry of noise and feathers. I reached for the eggs lying so snugly in the hay.

Suddenly the feeling of the night before came over me again. Something was waiting for me here. Calmly, easily, it was waiting. I had almost found it in the night sounds from the porch: it was almost here in the smooth roundness of the white eggs in my hand.

Out through the window, over toward the purple scar of hills, the sky was lightening through the mists. The sun was on its way. The small mountain out beyond the pasture, loomed blue-black in its closeness.

"Gert," I called. "Gert, does the little mountain out there have a name?"

Her voice came above the sharp jets of milk beginning in the second pail. "Hit's called Overlook. We climb it lots of times."

"Is there a path up it?"

"We wore a path up hit."

Quickly I went back over the hay, the can of eggs held carefully in my hand. "Gert, I want to climb **Overlook** before breakfast. Do you mind?"

"We don't mind. It ain't high and breakfast ain't till Pa sets the bath tubs out."

"Ain't no butter fer breakfast nohow," Dorkie said gloomily. "Sundays hit goes to the preacher."

But I hardly heard her. I was across the barn yard, latching the gate behind me, running along the fence path that led to the pasture.

"Path starts at the foot of the well," Gert stood in the door of the barn and called after me. I kept on running. The mists were clearing quickly now. I must reach the top of Overlook before the sun did.

The path turned at the well and went sharply up the side of the mountain. It was worn smooth from years of climbing. Big white boulders gleamed against the grayness of the earth, the path wound and curved between the rocks and trees.

The climbing was slower as the path narrowed and the mountain grew steeper. My throat was dry and parched. Scrub oak and rough bushes grew between the lichen-covered stones and huge boulders. Once my sweater caught and tore when I yanked it free without stopping.

Then the path sloped out ahead, the big pine on the top stood stretching its knotty arms against the horizon, and I reached it and sank breathlessly at its foot. The sun was rising from the mountain range beyond, past the valley below me, and it was huge and burning, a great golden mass of light. It stood poised on the mountain top for a moment. Slowly my breath came back, and the sky grew lighter and lighter, as the sun began its slow climb in the sky. Its long golden fingers reached over the hills and the valleys, gathering the rest of the mists from the earth. Beneath me the gray checkerboards of fields became shining green rows of corn, red-brown squares of new-turned earth, green and brown rows of strawberry fields. Houses gleamed gray-white on the distant hills. The white spire of the church reached through the trees at the right. The creek wound silver-gray in its bed; the dusty road traveled between thick shrubbery and tall trees.

Directly below me, by the timber line, was one of the square colorless farmhouses. A man was drawing water from the well; the screech of the iron pulley came faintly up to where I sat. A little girl in a pink dress came running from the barn. A woman followed, milk pails in her hands.

A surge in my heart made me want to shout to someone. I wanted to stand on my mountain and shout as long as I could.

I stood by the pine tree and cupped my hands to my mouth.

"Halllllooooo!" I shouted to the house below.

No answer but the echo from the ridge beyond.

"Halllooooo!" I called again.

"Halloo!" was a faint reply.

The little girl was still romping in the yard with her dog. She hadn't looked up. The woman had gone in the house, the man was emptying his bucket of water in the trough.

"Hello," I said, to whomever might be on the other side of the tree.

"Hello."

I smelled pipe smoke.

"Oh, Mr. MacCreighton," I said breathlessly. I sank down at the foot of the pine tree again. "For a moment I was almost frightened."

"They couldn't hear you," his voice said. "It's the Higgins family. They're deaf mutes."

"I didn't know."

The pungent smell of pipe smoke drifted lazily on the morning air. The sun was growing warmer. Quietness lay on the fields and houses in the valley. Neither Mr. MacCreighton nor I had words, and we sat there for a long time on either side of the tree. The mellowness of the sun made me feel part of the earth, the sky, the solidity of the crusted trunk at my back.

Finally Mr. MacCreighton spoke. "Where did the line come from about 'the golden rain of the sun's veins'?"

In a moment I roused myself to answer. "I don't remember. Father would have placed it. I was lost somewhere trying to remember a line about cat-clouds creeping across the sky. There are cat-clouds this morning."

He chuckled softly. "All this hour to find a thought as profound as that?"

"It isn't a day for profundity. That eased itself in when I wasn't thinking anything at all." In a moment I said, "It was from *Zarathustra*. He called them 'stealthy cats of prey.' I've always wondered why."

"Perhaps you didn't read enough of it. Who set you to reading *Zarathustra*?"

"No one did. Father read some of the lines to me once because they were pretty. The cat-clouds was one of them. I loved the line, 'And oft have I longed to pin them fast with the jagged gold-wires of lightning, that I might, like the thunder, beat the drum upon their kettle-bellies.'"

"Why?"

"Why what?"

"Why beat on their kettle-bellies?"

I laughed. "I think you're right—I didn't read far enough. I never bothered to find out why. I only loved the line."

He said, "Reminds me of the time I was in Florence and went to the Ufizzi Gallery to see Botticelli's *Venus*. I was homesick, so all I saw were the cattails in the bottom left hand corner. I caught the next boat home."

Of a sudden I wondered why I had never asked how he came here, before. Someway he had belonged here as Father had—part of this land and these people, yet only because he chose to come. "Was Granite Hill your home?"

"Home was in Kansas then," he answered. He knocked the pipe against the trunk of the tree. Burnt ashes were acrid in the air. "It's a little strange how I found this place," he went on. "An old fisherman on the St. Lawrence River told me about it. I don't know how he ever got there, or how I happened to find him, but it brought me here." It seemed a long time before he went on. "Funny thing about that church of mine in Lawrence, too. It was my first church. I was just out of school. It was the church that I had dreamed of preaching for since the first time I started studying for the ministry—yet when I began preaching all the words that I had stored up for years, I found myself shouting myself hoarse against a stone wall. Two years of it and I was still standing in front of a stone wall. Then I went fishing and found the fisherman."

"He sent you here?"

"He told me that the preacher at Granite Hill had died that spring. I wrote my letter here that night." He said, "I think I wrote the letter because of one thing the man said, 'Me, now, I steer clear of men with smartness,' he said. 'They think it's their reason for living when it ain't nothin' but their excuse for living.' I wanted to come find out what he meant."

"You found it here?"

"I found it working here. Now that I know what he was trying to say, I feel ready to go anywhere—any pulpit. But I don't want to go now." The brown hand with the bony wrist reached out from the other side of the tree and pointed to the valley below. "See Old Man Minch in his shack by the creek?"

"I can hear him," I laughed. Faintly up from the valley came a rasping voice singing a hymn.

"Old Man Minch is my deadline. He's drunk as a coot today, and he'll always be drunk as a coot—so I've sworn to stay until he cuts down to one jug of corn liquor a week, and quits spitting tobacco juice in the well every time he gets mad at Ella. An ever-receding deadline."

I pointed to the road nearer the creek. "I see two more of your congregation backsliding, too. Looks like you'll stay forever." Two little boys were scuffing up the dusty road, fishing poles over their shoulders, a few small fish swinging from a string.

John MacCreighton said, "There's Willie Moore to fall back on, too. He's supposed to ring the church bell right after milking, and he's gone back to sleep again this morning. The bell was to ring at seven."

"It couldn't be seven yet," I said.

A watch clicked open, then shut again. "It's a quarter after seven. Looks like I ring it again this morning." There was a scuffing of small sticks as he rose to his feet on the other side of the tree. "It has to ring extra long this morning. Not everyone knows the new teacher has come."

I took one last look at the valley below—the long morning shadows, the disappearing figures of the boys with the fishing poles, the sound of Old Man Minch's drunken hymns settling on the stillness. There was peace in the valley.

"I wish we never had to leave," I said. "The world will never stand still like this again."

I turned around the pine tree and John MacCreighton and I stood face to face. For the first time the length and breadth of him swept over me, the world of him burned in my body. He stood tall above me, waiting for me.

"A long time from now our roads may meet down there to make one," he said.

I nodded. "Yes," I said.

He turned and went down the path, down the mountainside, and I followed. His path left mine at the pasture well. His went across the field, over the stile to the woods and the spire of the church beyond. I watched until his long hard stride was out of sight. Then I turned up the path along the fence. My answer was full in me now: one year—three years—five years—what did it matter how long it took to walk to the dream that had always been with me? It was still there. I had been born in it. What really mattered was finding my own excuse for living—knowing my excuse for living. To walk my own path, free, with an eye to see things as they are. . . .

Who had said that? Father? Somewhere, someone had said those words to me.

"To sing, to laugh, to dream—to walk in my own way and be alone, free, with an eye to see things as they are—"

It was from *Cyrano de Bergerac*. But it was Mother who used to repeat it to us.

> "To travel any road
> Under the sun, under the stars, nor doubt
> If fame or fortune lie beyond the bourne—"

I could hear Mother in the kitchen now, sliding the pan of cornbread into the oven, calling into the living-room while I practiced. "Mary, the notes on that page aren't blobs of ink! Sing them—it's a song—" "Well, Mother, I heard Mrs. Alcock play it this way on her recital in Little Rock last year—"

"Don't play it anyone else's way, Sister. Sing your own song—"

"Never to make a line I have not heard in my own heart—"

Father's shoulder back of mine as we sat on the swing and watched Arcturus in a sky littered with stars. "Teaching comes from here, Mary," touching my chest, "not here," pointing to my hands.

"Teacher—Teacher—"

Dorkie was running down the path from the house, her Sunday dress starched and white around her. "Teacher, hit's most church time. Ye missed breakfast. Air ye aimin' to go to church?"

She stopped just beyond me. I looked at her standing there in the sunlight. She cocked her head at me, puzzled.

"Air ye comin', Teacher?"

The church bell had begun to ring in the distance. The tones hung silver and trembling in my throat. "Of course I'm coming, Dorkie." I held out my hand. "Come on—run with me."

She hesitated. "I got on new shoes."

I laughed breathlessly. "You won't fall."

She put her hand in mine and we ran down the path, up at the pasture gate, up the hill to the square white house. The hill was steep and the path was full of stones, but Dorkie didn't slip. Not once. I had her hand and she was laughing.